CROM CRUACH

VALKYRIE LOUGHCREWE

Featuring Illustrations by Echo Echo
Cover Art by Jonathan LaMantia

*Content warnings are available at the end of this book. Please consult this
list for any particular subject matter you may be sensitive to.*

TENEBROUS

PRESS

Production of this novel was made possible in part by a grant from the Regional Arts & Culture Council. Visit https://racc.org/ for more information.

Published by Tenebrous Press.
Visit our website at www.tenebrouspress.com.

First Printing, September 2022.

Print ISBN: 978-1-7379823-2-6
eBook ISBN: 978-1-7379823-3-3

Cover art and design by Jonathan LaMantia.

Interior illustrations by Echo Echo.

Edited by Matt Blairstone with Alex Woodroe.

Formatting by Lori Michelle.

Map by Dewi Hargreaves

Supplementary Material by Matt Blairstone & Valkyrie Loughcrewe

Printed in the United States of America.

CROM CRUACH startled me. We might need to invent a new genre for them, like *Anarcho-Folk Splatter* or *Lyrical Black-Metal Horror*. If you don't want to read a novella mixing ancient occult horror with modern communal politics that's efficiently and viscerally detailed . . . well then, I really don't know how to help you."

—**Joe Koch**, author of *The Wingspan of Severed Hands*

A family is found slaughtered in their home, yet their corpses still move; committed to the routine of their daily lives, heedless of their own grisly deaths. A local occultist commune is suspected of the crime. The bloody legacy of Catholicism and the dark roots of ancient paganism intertwine in the aftermath of a recent national revolution.

Welcome to the Ireland of tomorrow.

Two ex-Gardai officers, a former Franciscan monk and a young trans woman race to determine the cause of the slayings before tensions in the community boil over and kick off a new Satanic Panic, driving the tenuous fledgling nation back into the arms of the Church.

CROM CRUACH is a distinctly Irish anxiety piece about the reluctant future and repressed past of a country trying to shrug off the shackles of colonialism, wrapped in the shiny black leather of *Giallo* and written in a hallucinatory, poetic style fit for the fog-shrouded mysticism of the emerald isle.

"Loughcrewe plunges the reader head first into a skillful mix of folkloric, speculative and human horror. It left me breathless at every turn; afraid to turn the page, afraid not to. It's not hyperbole to say I finished this with my mouth hanging open, my heart alight with horror and my mind afire with possibility. An incredible read."

—**Laurel Hightower**, author of *Crossroads* and *Below*

ALSO FROM TENEBROUS PRESS:

Green Inferno: The World Celebrates Your Demise
edited by Matt Blairstone

In Somnio: A Collection of Modern Gothic Horror
edited by Alex Woodroe

Your Body is Not Your Body edited by Alex Woodroe
and Matt Blairstone

One Hand to Hold, One Hand to Carve by M.Shaw

Lure by Tim McGregor

Dedicated to all Irish Republican Socialists who have been, are currently, or will be incarcerated by free state or British authorities.

Also dedicated to the spirit of the crossroads, who some would call The Devil.

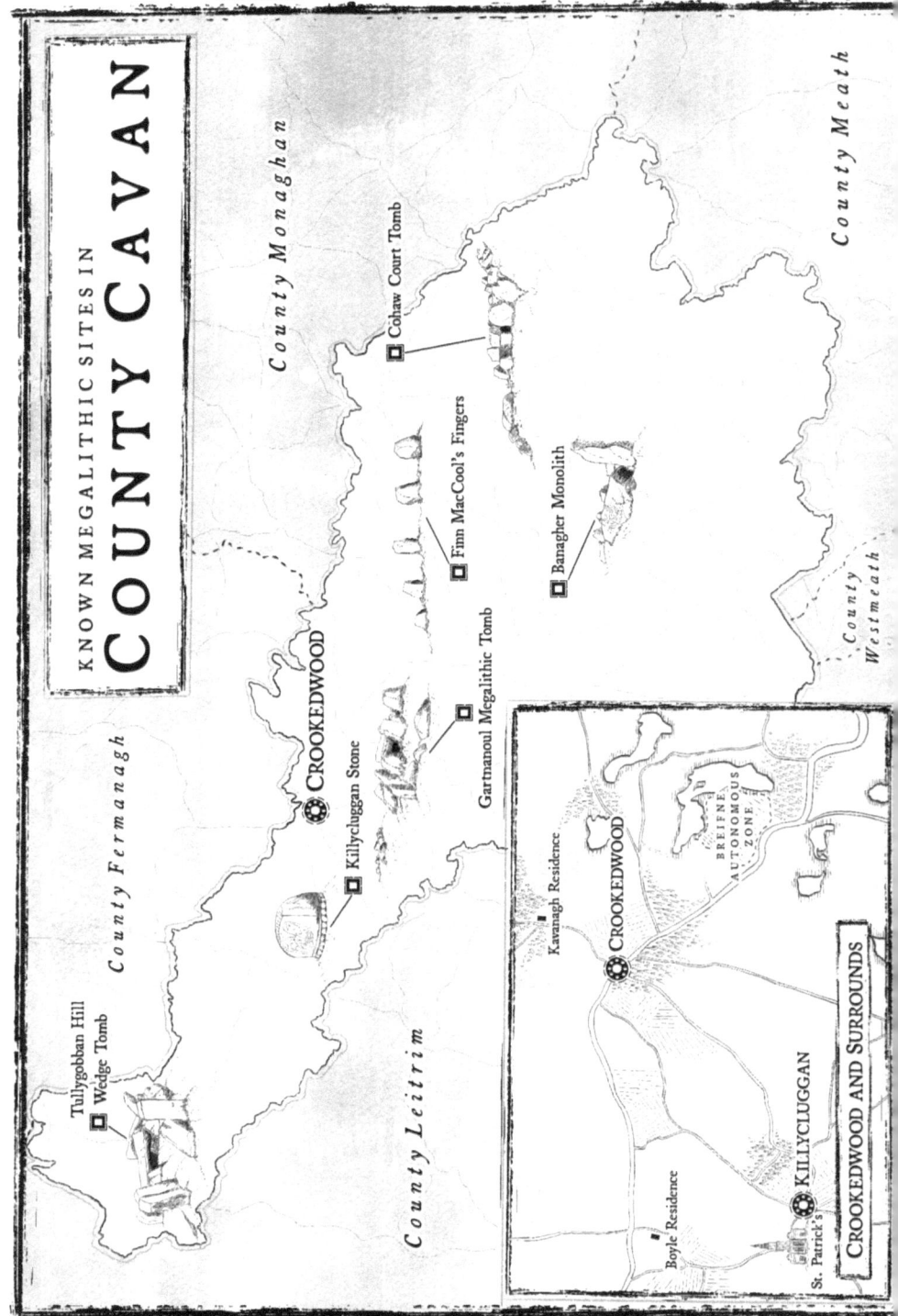

KNOWN MEGALITHIC SITES IN
COUNTY CAVAN

County Monaghan

County Meath

County Fermanagh

County Leitrim

County Westmeath

● CROOKEDWOOD

■ Killycluggan Stone

■ Tullygobban Hill Wedge Tomb

■ Gartnanoul Megalithic Tomb

■ Finn MacCool's Fingers

■ Banagher Monolith

■ Cohaw Court Tomb

CROOKEDWOOD AND SURROUNDS

● CROOKEDWOOD

BREIFNE AUTONOMOUS ZONE

■ Kavanagh Residence

● KILLYCLUGGAN

■ Boyle Residence

St. Patrick's

CROM CRUACH
PART ONE

CHAPTER 1

In a high, tamed place of power,
on a fog-strewn darkened hill,
the parish chapel burns.
Seen all the way from town,
devouring light of flames,
flickering over silent graves.

A gathering mass of figures,
masks of sackcloth, paper, wicker,
stand like a famine procession,
along a polluted river,
flowing from a dying city far away
from this rural midnight mob.

An old man in an ancient car stops along his journey home,
steps out onto cracked tarmac,
he cannot smell the fragrant night air.
Senses dulled from fags and drink,
he stares, red eyed,
down across the valley, lined with sitka spruce.
Like a beacon burns the chapel,
he balls his fists and spits a curse.

The world has left me lost and dying!
He dares not,
dares not,
think.

Miles away on down the road,

VALKYRIE LOUGHCREWE

but not as far as town,
a young lad, Gearoid Boyle, asleep,
floats upward from his bed,
lit only by a crack of light.
His mother Lynda stands,
a shadow in the doorway,
eyes widening in fright.

The parish priest,
expelled,
runs from his house toward his car.
Pebbles pelting outward from the dancing shadows, set
in a blasphemous orange blaze,
the masked congregation jeers.
He had himself a gun, but he left it in the house,
couldn't turn it on his parishfolk.
It would be right to die for christ.

And death does stalk this night.

Miles away on down the road,
but not as far as town,
along a tarmacadam path,
lit solely by the clouded moonlight
glinting off a butcher's knife,
gripped by black gloved archetypal death,
indeed does stalk this night.

Lynda racing down the stairs,
lightbulbs flickering overhead.
She wants to scream, but breath is caught,
an image burned into her mind,
of a boy,
unhooked from gravity.

The lights go out and her foot misplaces,
gravity still her master,
and she falls
to the cold tiled floor of the hall.

CROM CRUACH

By the front door,
an apparition in the dark,
marked by ice blue glowing eyes,
a phantom hag.

Its outline visible to Lynda's streaming eyes
even in the pitch black freezing,
Lynda screams,
stirring Padraig.
She hears him bolt awake in frantic panicking, upstairs.

The hag is gone, the lights back on
Lynda's lying on the floor
pain coursing through her lower body
and the front door handle turns.

He stands outside,
figure in black.
Nowhere near the door,
between the pillars at the driveway's end.

Gloved hand outstretched
and grasping, turns
the mechanism of the locked front door
releasing to his will at distance

as firefighting volunteers
start arriving on the scene
of the burning of the church.

They fight the blaze,
the masked marauding band long gone,
now only a gaggle of onlookers remain.

A cry is heard from the roadside,
exalted on a cloud of weed smoke,

"It's about damn time!"

VALKYRIE LOUGHCREWE

And a ways on down the road, but not as far as town,
the dark stranger in his coat and hat
fills the frame of the front door,
as Padraig barrels down the stairs,
his trusty hurley in his hand,
he takes a mighty swing
to no avail.

The weapon splinters as it hits,
So unbothered is the dread intruder
that the hat stays undisturbed
upon his head.

Cold leather glove on Padraig's throat,
pressure applied to crush the trachea,
and steel, in rapid thrusting motions,
breaks his flitting eyelids.
Jabbing into jelly,
left right left right
drop
he hits the floor.

And Lynda's crawling now.
Fingers reach across the threshold
of the door,
touch the bristles of the mat,
when the killer's heavy boot
comes slamming down upon her skull.

Brain to leaking pulp,
Bone to splintered shards.
A headless body at the open door,
eyeless one upon the stairs.

No trace of any killer,
Gearoid's room sits dark and still
as embers of the blazing church sing smoke into the clouds.

CROM CRUACH

Above the county they call Cavan,
regal Meath's sinister twin,
where ancient bogland rots in silence
over sunken burial mounds.

CHAPTER 2

There's sunlight streaming in now
from the Boyles' open door,
down the stairs from landing windows,
and through the archway of the living room,
with its cheap wall-mounted flatscreen
and its fancy leather couch.

Lynda and Padraig have gone missing,
but the pulp and blood's still there.

Standing in the hallway, a pair of uniformed Gardaí.
A grizzled older fella, jaw set, shotgun in his hand
and a younger chap,
young Fine Gaeler head on him, of course,
grips a metal bat,
not looking all that brave or confident
this morning.

The radio is on,
the sound drifting from the kitchen.

"Hello, Lynda, Padraig? Gearoid?
Anyone around?"

The older fella, Marco, calls out,
receiving no response,
from the still, bucolic house,
as robins trill their song outside.

CROM CRUACH

"We should call for backup,"
Iarla, the younger Garda suggests.

"What backup could there be?"

"You know, Terry and the boys?"

"We don't need those cunts.
We're still the police, now check upstairs,
I'll check the kitchen."

"I don't wanna go up there alone, Marco."

Marco grunts and offers his gun to his young and worried ward,
who hesitates, the balance of their microcosm off.
The bigger, gruffer man passing the superior arm to him?

"Hand me that fucking bat,"

He growls and Iarla takes the gun,

"And get up them fuckin' stairs."

They go their separate ways.
Iarla, shaking, up the steps,
trying not to look down
at the dried black bloody streaks
of last night's gore.

Marco steps into the living room,
which reeks of potpourri,
and notices a faint trace
of bloody footprints on the floor.

They trail across the carpet,
lead to a half opened doorway,
tiled floor visible on the other side.
Marco guesses it's the kitchen.

VALKYRIE LOUGHCREWE

A sudden THUNK from that room,
the forceful slamming of a cupboard door,
confirms two things for Marco
that he's not all that pleased to know.

The first thing being—yes, it's most probably a kitchen,
and the second being—no, he and the boy are not alone.

"Ah Jaysus,"

Marco mutters to himself,
regretting handing off his weapon to the younger lad upstairs,
who himself has heard
the eerie thumping coming from the kitchen,
but his orders given stand,
and he fears the reprimanding
that Marco would administer
if he dallied from his task.

So he moves toward a landing door that's open but a crack,
a bookshelf he can see and blood
spattered on the floor
as if some animal or . . . otherwise
had been butchered in that room.

Worse still he hears a sound
just beyond the limits of his sight.
A squeaking, like an office chair.
He grips his shotgun tight.

Downstairs Marco,
rounding toward the kitchen,
is aware of an unsettling sound of
sloshing, spilling liquid
around the corner.

He finds himself surprised to see
Padraig Boyle, in his underwear,

CROM CRUACH

blood caked across his pallid skin
pouring milk into a china bowl.

Cereal boxes overturned,
shreddies scattered on the counter,
milk overflowing from the brim of Padraig's bowl,
and Iarla screams upstairs, diverting Marco's attention.

He looks back for a moment
and when his sight returns to Padraig
the man of the house is facing him,
pouring milk onto the floor.

His eyes are gone,
the sockets shredded,
skin as pale as death, as milk.

"Padraig, what happened to you?!" Marco cries out
as Padraig lumbers, blind, toward him,
scooping up his heaping bowl of cereal
on the way.

There's a chill off him, like a freezer's open door.

Marco flinches in revulsion,
sidestepping Padraig as he shambles past
paying Marco no attention.

"P-padraig?"

Iarla's storming down the stairs
calling Marco's name, hysterically,
about to burst in and see
the eyeless body of a murder victim
flop down onto the couch,
spilling shreddies everywhere,
and fumble for the remote control
like he was never even killed.

CHAPTER 3

The morning dew settles
on a blackened,
burned out fire,
in the middle of a field,
littered with cans
and empty bottles.
Goran's back at the barbeque,
with fish caught from the lake, sizzling.
Despite the morning after vibes
the session's still ongoing.

Fionnuala's got the aux cord,
and the PA on the pallet stage
is blaring out the techno.
The people snoozing
in their tents,
are too chemically obliviated,
for the noise to wake them
from their slumber.

Podge Dunne and Oisin Hall
are throwing shapes
beside the barn,
jaws going ninety miles a minute,
last men standing,
undead shades.

CROM CRUACH

Fionnuala's face
has spittle caked
into the corners of her mouth.
Pale, greasy,
mobile phone DJ,
in the dim and hazy
light of another
abominable Monday.

Not a single brain cell left among them,
or those inside the tents,
or over at the Commune house,
bar those who had the sense to go to bed.

And there along the path,
down from the farmhouse,
comes a white van out through the mist
up to the barn.
It's Gerry and his aul boy Tom.

Podge grins and waves,
he saunters over,
somehow still
a little compos mentis,
but poor Oisin,
dead man standing,
barely upright but still grooving
to the beat set by Fionnuala
until she switches, callously,
to a new tune,
breaking the mood
and snapping Oisin
from his waking fugue.
He stands and looks at her aghast:

"Hey I was really into that."

She shrugs
and Oisin blinks, one eye at a time,

VALKYRIE LOUGHCREWE

as Podge lights up another herbal fag
and nods his head to Gerry who emerges
from the van.

"Well lad how's she cuttin'?"
 Podge Dunne cheerily exclaims.

"If yer not too shpaced out from last night would ye give us a
    hand loading up some hay?"
Gerry asks.

"No bother hai," Podge pipes back. "Is that your auld lad with ya
    there?"

"Aye, lookin forward to seeing the back of him but it does him
    good getting some fresh air."

"As sure he's a sound chap,"
Podge remarks,
"Morning Tom!"

Old white haired Tom waves lazily.
He's out, stretching the legs,
marvelling at the carnage
left by the revelry last night.

He eyeballs Oisin and Fionnula,
who cuts the tunes and calls it quits.

"Alright, an old white man's staring,
taking this as a sign to go to bed."

Oisin looks back at Tom,
who, in his Sunday best,
Seems to be regarding the young Fenian
with disdain.

Or maybe it's just Oisin,
projecting paranoia

CROM CRUACH

from deep inside his own
misfiring, speed-fried,
lizard brain.

"Do ya know Thin Lizzy do ya?" Tom asks with a half smile.

"Huh?" Oisin replies,
wondering if Tom's asking if he knows Thin Lizzy
just cause he's black?
Old guys are weird.

"Are ye on the beer, young lad?" The old man asks,
changing tack, but smirking gnomishly.

"Hell yeah I'm on the beer I'm on . . . all kindsa shit, wait . . .
    Who are you?"

Tom laughs and Goran, the early bird, calls out,

 "Breakfast's up, for those awake who want to have some eats!"

 Then, over from the house across, a sudden distant bellowing.

"Ah fuck," Goran laments, "That's Aidan starting up again."

"On who's FUCKING AUTHORITY!"

Bearded Aidan roars, red faced,
standing before Iarla and Marco,
who've only just arrived
the two lads since last we saw them
having changed out of their uniforms,
into civilian clothes,
and Marco's not all that delighted
with being berated so he goes:

"On the authority of common FUCKING SENSE, YOU DAFT
    PRICK!"
Squaring up, Iarla cowering behind him.

VALKYRIE LOUGHCREWE

Aidan looks delighted at the thought of
scrapping rightly
with this self inflated prick
who's nostalgic for the day when
An Garda Siochana still existed,
when he still possessed the power
to throw people into cages.

When there were laws in place to punish
lads like red faced Aidan.
If he were to get into a fight
and let slip a concealed knife,
Stick it between two ribs
and twist and in combat,
take a Garda's life.

But this is not the time or place for any sort of fight.

First thing in the morning,
right in front of the gaff,
filled with sleeping permaculturists,
and general rave riff raff.

Every single one of them
having seen their fill of violence in their lives,
this party supposed to take their minds
off all that kinda shite.

The standoff seems set to just drag on indefinitely,
until a window on the second floor
pops open with a bang
and it's the scraggy head of Saoirse Kavanagh,
the communal gaff's first owner,
who inhales dramatically
before erupting in a fervor,

"SHUT THE FUCK UP THE LOT OF YEZ PEOPLE ARE TRYING
TO FUCKING SLEEP YA FUCKIN WRECKHEADS!"

CROM CRUACH

Aidan smirks, lowering his voice.

"You gonna arrest me, Marco? Go on, I'd love to see you try."

Marco goes to speak,
but then the front door opens,
and Jimmy Candon
steps out onto the gravel
with a long and sharp machete.

"What da fuck's goin on out here lads?"

"These wankers think they're still the Gards," Aidan snorts,
    conspiratorially.

"Aidan's drunk out of his mind and trying to drive off into town,"
Marco sighs, calming his tone out of respect and fear of Jimmy.

"I've gotta work, man,"
Aidan pleads his case.
"People gotta eat, I gotta pull my weight."

"Shoulda thought of that before you woke up pissed,"
Iarla mutters from behind his meat shield.

"Fuck did you just say to me ya prick?"

"Aidan, I'll cover your shift mate, go off to bed," Jimmy offers
    reluctantly.

"Jimmy, I'm going down there to get people fed."

Jimmy steps up toward Aidan.
The two men lock eyes intensely,
Jimmy's next few words
come delivered in such a manner,
that Aidan knows there will be no recourse
than to just accept his fate.

VALKYRIE LOUGHCREWE

"Well, I'll fuckin' drive ya down then," Jimmy says
and spins round on his heel.
He points his blade in the direction
of the two ex lawmen in his yard.

"And what are you two boys doing at our fine establishment
so early in the morning?"

"We're looking for Oisin Hall."

Jimmy points his blade over
at the path toward the barn,
where a small crowd of folks have gathered,
watching the early morning drama.
Oisin's swaying there among them
sleep deprived and barely able to
keep himself upright.

"There he is there, will yiz be leaving now?"

CHAPTER 4

Oisin flops into the back of the car.
It's not a Garda cruiser, just your average sedan.
He lies across the back seat and falls half asleep,
as soon as his body finds itself sideways.

"Bang of drink off ya man," Iarla remarks.

"Hey, it's Saturday," Oisin grumbles,
barely audible, his face buried in the seat.
He tries instinctively to pull his long jacket around him.
Some semblance of a blanket,
to send him off to sleep at last.

"Sorry to grab you up while you're going through it, pal,"
Marco adopts a fatherly tone.
"But it's a pretty serious emergency."

Oisin, aching to lose consciousness,
drags himself up into an awkward sit,
wondering why the hell these two ex-cops
have come to him, of all people.

"Oh Jesus, what is it?" He groans.

Marco starts up the car and pulls away,
heading down the idyllic lane.

"Let's get out of this den of iniquity first.
Also, lad, It's Monday."

VALKYRIE LOUGHCREWE

As rough and pockmarked
as the lane may be which winds
away from the commune,
toward town,
the motion,
and the earthy smell,
of the inside of the old sedan
knocks Oisin right to sleep.

He briefly dreams of a lazy bright river,
a body lying face down in the trickling green water,
stuck between a pair of rocks,
when he's dragged back into waking
by the sound of Marco's voice.

"Have you had any word from her?"

Oisin wakes to find himself
face pressed against the window.
He pulls away,
leaving a regrettable greasy stain
upon the glass.

They're parked up at a petrol station,
dotted round with signs, giving all of the information
about when it's shutting down, and a handy dandy URL
on how to transition into life without a car that runs on gas.

"N-no . . . She's deleted all social media. It's . . . weird. I'm
     worried."

"Well you're not the only one. People have started wondering . . . "

"Wondering? About Dace?"

"Oisin, the Boyle family were murdered in their home last night."

"What?"

CROM CRUACH

"Padraig and Lynda Boyle are dead, their son Gearoid is missing."

"I-I don't know them, Marco, I'm sorry."

"No mention of them among your satanist friends?"

"Oh, come on man, they're not satanists, they're just—"

"Church burners? Killers? Lawless violent thugs?"

"Oh man, I don't know anything about that church fire.
It's not like this is the only county that craic is happening in.
And I heard that it was some aul folks who drove that priest out of his house.
Anyway, all of those pagan types were partying down at the farm last night!"

"All night? You sure about that? You don't look like you're a state to remember much of anything from last night."

"Look, Marco, this isn't some satanic panic cult shite goin' on, it's just—
Wait—are you and Iarla the only ones who know about this murder?
You've gotta tell the CDA."

"I will!" Marco bellows.
A sudden, frustrated bark.
He takes a breath to calm his nerves.

"I will tell them. We just first have to . . . "
He trails off, grimacing,
steeling himself for what comes next.

"You're still a Catholic, Oisin? You still go to mass?"

"Yeah and I'm not too thrilled about the local going up in flames, if that's what you're getting at."

VALKYRIE LOUGHCREWE

"Grand. Okay."
Marco looks distressed.
He grasps in vain to find the right words.

"When you were with the Franciscans,
did you ever hear anything about murder victims' bodies . . .
Not quite staying dead?

"Wait so, they're not dead? I'm not following."

Marco hisses as if in pain, pinches the bridge of his nose,
and Iarla chooses the worst possible time
to open up the passenger door,
and slide into the car,
with a tray of petrol station coffees
and a box of donut holes.

"They didn't have oat milk, Marco, so I got you soy instead."

Marco turns to look at Iarla, eyes bulging wide in flustered rage.

"Iarla," he pauses for effect, "shut da fuck up."

Iarla blushes, and sets the tray down.
Marco turns back to face Oisin.

"The corpses are moving, Oisin,
Without eyes. Without a head.
Walking around the house like it's night of
the living bloody dead."

"Are you . . . serious?" Oisin stammers.

Iarla whispers, fearful,

"Yes."

Marco pinches the bridge of his nose again,
shuts his eyes.

CROM CRUACH

"It does seem to be a factor in this awful fucking day."
He sighs.

"I've never heard anything like that, outside of,
folk tales maybe but even then . . . "

"Can you do an exorcism, Oisin? Just make whatever it is stop?
Before we go to those pri—to the Community Defence
    Association.
Before anyone else finds out."

"I know . . . some things about banishing
and removing hauntings, I mean,
but . . . they're like, zombies?
Are they violent?"

"They were just . . . walking around the gaff like nothing had
    happened," Iarla says.
"I'm afraid they might get out and wander off."

Oisin's mouth is open, he's looking all around,
trying to process this bizarre influx of information,
when he spots his cousin Karl heading out of the station
with a box of assorted sweets,
toward his battered old red van.

"Did you restrain them?" Oisin asks,
looking back to see Marco,
temporarily distracted by his snacks.

"They're not going anywhere," Marco says,
somewhat ironically,
as this will be the moment
where Oisin makes his move.
He bursts out of the unlocked door
and races toward Karl,
who's starting up his van,
and humming along to the radio.

VALKYRIE LOUGHCREWE

Iarla opens up his door but Marco grabs his shoulder.

"Don't you fucking move."

The ex Gardai watch dumbfounded,
as Oisin throws himself in front
of a battered red van.
He leaps into the passenger seat
and the driver hits the gas, no questions asked,
top speed as quick as it can reach it,
And the van goes screeching off.

"What the fuck is he doing?" Iarla snarls
with all the fearsomeness of a juvenile labrador.

"He's high, he's paranoid, and we just
freaked him the fuck out."

"Shit, oh shit. They're gonna think—"

"They're gonna find us waiting for 'em
in a house that's full of zombies.
Assuming he tells them what we told him,
that will give us some leverage to plead our case."

"I don't wanna go back there."

"If the CDA catch you at home
before they can verify our story
they'll kick the living shit out of you."

"Then I'll go somewhere else?
Don't make me go back there, man."

"Are you bailin' on me, here?"

"Marco, please."

CROM CRUACH

"You bail on me for this one, and
it's over. You think Mrs. Cahill is
going to ever be able to leave the
house again if she thinks the town
is overrun with violent anarchists?
What do you think Stanley and Niall
and Fergus are going to do when
they hear that there's no order
left in this town?"

"I'm not quitting, Marco, I'm just—"

"Oh, you're not quitting, great.
Boyle house it is."

Iarla looks like he's about to cry.

"Where are we going, Iarla?"

"Boyle's house it is, sargeant."

***

Oisin shifts his body, trying to minimize
the destruction he has wrought upon his cousin's
heaping box of sweets and crisps,
that he sat straight down on in a panic.

"I'm so fuckin' sorry Karl!"

"You look high as shit! What the fuck man?"

"I was just abducted by Marco Higgins and Iarla McFuckface!"

"Iarla the garda?"

"I think they killed some people."

"I wouldn't be surprised, fucking pigs. Are you joking?"

VALKYRIE LOUGHCREWE

Oisin manages to get all of the ruined junk food
up onto his lap, scanning the mirrors frantically
to see if they're being followed.

"No man, they told me some weird
story about how they think the Morrighannain
murdered the Boyle family, whoever they are.
They wanted me to come with them
to do an exorcism on some
zombies or some shit."

"Man you're tripping.
What the fuck is a Morgonawn?"

"You know, that little pagan group who live
up outside of Breifne? On the farm?"

"Saoirse and Aaron and them, yeah.
Is that what they call themselves?"

"Not everyone up there, just the few that—
Look, people are dead, man!
I think—I think Iarla and Marco wanted to get me alone
so they could torture me or
something. I think people are
really fucked off about the church
burnings and they're blaming the
Morrigh—Jimmy and them.
I am high, yes.
I was sessioning last night,
and the cops just plucked me out of
the gaff this morning."

"They're not the cops any more, Oisin."

"Try telling them that."

Karl sighs, pulls out his phone,

starts dialing the number he hoped he'd never have to
outside of poker night or five-a-side.

"Alright, we're taking this to Jimmy."

"Fuck sake, no, Jimmy's asleep man.
He was out last night.
He'll go nuts."

"And what about when he finds out
you were too much of a chickenshit
to wake him up and tell him about a
fucking murder?"

There's a pause as Jimmy's phone starts to ring out.

"The whole Boyle family?"
Karl asks his cousin.

"That's what they said, although
they said Gearoid is missing?
I don't know him."

"I've met him. He's in school with
Saoirse's sister. I took them up to
some art gallery in Kells in
October for a school trip."

"Right, do you thi—"

Beep
Jimmy's picked up.
Karl doesn't give him a chance to complain.

"Jimmy, there's been a mass fucking murder, mate."

Organization, known as **The Morrighannain**, openly practices pagan rituals and offers workshops on occult practices, alternative farming and craftwork to the local community. A more sinister hidden agenda of ritualism and occultism beneath the public facade is suspected.

Contact with local drug manufacturers is confirmed, as is their conduction of "educational seminars" on psychedelic drug use. Relationship to the local paramilitary police (see separate entry: *the CDA*) is somewhat strained, but there is overlap in membership.

OBSERVED MEMBERSHIP OF THE MORRIGHANNAIN

Dace Vitkus - Lithuanian National. Uncertain if she partook in the Overthrow of Democracy in the British Isles. Possible post war economic migrant. Though the group claims to be non-hierarchical, Vitkus seems to be a clear leader in the group's spiritual and ritual activities. Possible blackmail potential if family can be located.

Jimmy Candon - Irish Traveller, but unrelated to the local Traveller Community as far as can be determined. As such, it is likely Candon is on the run, perhaps in debt or due to criminal activity. Possible homosexual with blackmail potential. Trained enemy combatant from the Overthrow of Democracy in the British Isles. Active CDA member.

Leanne Conaty - Trained enemy combatant from the Overthrow of Democracy in the British Isles. Internet presence reaching back to 2003, public interest in "ghost hunting" and occultism. Artist, soap maker. Doesn't seem to be an active CDA member. Could be a potential limited capacity asset.

Goran Bašić - Former Catholic Priest in Bosnia. Arrival in Ireland seems timed specifically to take part in the Overthrow of Democracy. Trained Enemy Combatant. Possibly fled Bosnia, possible criminal ties/Blackmail potential. Rumored interest in Demonology, po████ ████ving the grou█ to Satanist activity. CDA status uncertai█

███ "Saoirse" Kavanagh - Traine█ enemy co████████ of Democracy in the British Isles. Openly Homo/Transsexu██ relationship with family indicates low blackmail potential, █ ███████████ may be useful for ████████ Active CDA member.
Son of Fintan Kavanagh: wealthy and influential before the Overthr█ of Democracy, and colluded with the dissidents. Has access to land █ property, including the property the cult is residing on.

Aidan Cronan - Longest history of involvement with Dissident Republican Activity and vigilantism of any group member. See attached arrest record (file #4). Active if not founding/leading CDA member and Trained Enemy Combatant. Extremely dangerous and well connected to the broader communist militant network. Most useful as a target of

Terry Collier - Member of the Ordo Templi Orientis of Irela█ inside that organisation will be able to provide easy inf████ █er. Trained Enemy Combatant and active CDA member. Au████ ████hedelic Drug Culture and OTO history. Potential t████ ██████████ if required.

CHAPTER 5

Fintan Kavanagh's made it home,
exhausted, at long last.
Though his body is warped by time, and conflict,
he drags this heavy object that he cannot see.
It twists his back,
and he knows somehow behind him,
that he's leaving a trail of blood,
but also that he isn't bleeding.

He struggles through the hallway,
into the comfort of the kitchen,
lit by sunshine through the patio doors.
Little Ray is sitting at the table.
He's smiling.

Fintan's wife, Louise, is beside him,
dressed in the same finery that she wore
on the day of her mother's funeral.

Norrie's there as well,
seated on the other side,
wearing nothing, naked, sweating, panting,
like the night of Ray's conception.

And they're all together and they're happy,
still Fintan feels this thing behind him
that he dare not lose his grip on,
though it feels like his arm's about to break.

VALKYRIE LOUGHCREWE

"How'd the day go?"
He finds himself asking the trio at the table.

"Did you talk to them?" Norrie asks,
 her voice calmer than
 her appearance would suggest

"I did. I stopped them. This was before," he responds,
suddenly uncertain what day it is.

"It wasn't before this dinner," Ray says absentmindedly.
"They're coming back now, daddy."

The doorbell rings
and Fintan's latent dread explodes.
A blizzard in his innards.
He loses grip of the shining,
bleeding sword he drags with him,
everywhere he ever goes,
just out of sight, and out of mind.

The sound of the bell elongates,
distorting, overwhelming,
it's resonance transforming
the comfort of the kitchen.

And Fintan's falling backwards,
into a familiar metal chair,
in a cold garage,
and *oh god,*
they've bound my hands
with barbed wire.
God no no, the pliers.
I thought that this was over.
It's clamping down on Fintan's
last remaining fingernail.

"This is what you get."

CROM CRUACH

Fintan wakes up screaming,

"Norrie!"

On his nicotine stained couch again,
in a two day old suit,
In a room that reeks of giving up.
He cries out a couple of times,
for help,
to an empty echoing house.

"Saoirse! Sonia!"

His head is pounding.
The drink has failed to end his life again.
He reaches for his cane and
pulls himself upward,
creaking to his feet.

He hobbles to the cupboard and pulls out
a fresh decanter
from his endless hoard of alcohol.

Through the open kitchen door
there's someone sitting at the table.

Not Louise or Norrie, they're long gone,
one to heaven, one to Hong Kong,
she and Fintan's bastard son.
Nor is it Sonia.
Though she still lives here, technically,
he rarely ever sees her.

No, this is someone else,
her face half lost to shadow,
skin pale and splinter-marred,
jaw loose, hanging,
rotting, scarred,
fingers all broken into angles.

VALKYRIE LOUGHCREWE

Fintan opens the decanter,
starts his routine descent anew.

***

"I had a dream about my dad last night."

Saoirse cuddles with Cora in their well kept room.
Even though the ruckus outside has passed,
they still can't get back to sleep,
they're content to simply luxuriate,
in their mutual proximity,
under wall hung flags, both red and black,
and blue and pink and white.

A half finished jug of poitin,
sits beneath Saoirse's kalashnikov,
propped up in the corner of the room.

"Oof, ya wanna talk about it?"
Cora murmurs in her ear.

"I honestly don't remember anything about it,
just that he was there,
and he didn't seem like he was doing great."

"Go visit him, sure."

"Yeah, I should. He's . . .
Just . . .
Watching him fall into the bottle, it's..
Like, what the fuck do I do?
Take all the booze out of his house and hide his
car keys?"

"That first thing doesn't sound too
bad. My recommendation would be
that we go visit him first."

CROM CRUACH

Saoirse squirms around in the nest,
to face her smiling lover.

"We?" She asks, astonished.

"Yeah, why not?"

"Fuck it. It could be nice.
Might do him some good."

"Absolutely." Cora stretches.
"But I'm not getting out of bed today."

"God,
and I haven't had a catch up with
Sonia in like a month either.
And I should fucking call Ray
for fuck sake,
I'm terrible at being part of a family."

Cora goes to say something,
and is interrupted by
a rapping at the door.

"Piss off!" Saoirse groans.

"There's been a murder." Jimmy's voice.
"We're having a CDA meeting at McGuigan's in ten."

Cora bolts upward, Saoirse freezes,
staring wide eyed at the ceiling.

"Jesus Christ," Cora exclaims. "H-holy shit, who?"

You ask that like you're gonna know them,
she thinks bitterly to herself.

VALKYRIE LOUGHCREWE

"The Boyle's up in Crookedwood,"
comes the reply.
And sure enough,
she's never heard that name before.
Something uncomfortable and sour
twists deep inside her gut.

"Who's driving?" Saoirse asks.

"That's the issue, everyone's knackered,"
Jimmy says behind the door.

"I wouldn't trust meself behind the wheel this morning,
 to be honest."

"I'm good to drive, I slept,"
Saoirse says,
still staring at the ceiling.
Jimmy slaps the door,
startling the two women.

"Sound, see you two downstairs."

His footsteps thunder down the stairs.

"Ahh, no babe, stay in, I'll go."
Cora puts her arms around her partner.

"No way."

 Saoirse starts to rise.

"He said murder, I wanna know
who we've got to go fuck up."

CHAPTER 6

A wood of ash and oak,
dark clouds hang overhead.
The birds are brightly singing,
as Sonia trudges, cautiously,
off the path, toward a breaking of the tree line,
out into a cattle field.

Across the road stands Saint Patrick's
grand cathedral, spires rising
from the placid countryside,
atop Killycluggin hill.

She steels herself,
and marches on cautiously,
so as to not disturb the skittish cows.
Still, quick enough. Gearoid is waiting,
and she knows not what he might do
if she leaves him for too long in solitude.

Away on past the road,
and up the winding, white gravel path,
to the grand cathedral.

Sonia ducks in through the open doors
and stops there at the font.
She stays still there for a moment,
looks back down the gravel path.
There's nobody approaching,
no sound of anyone inside.

Regardless, she's going to
have to do this fast.

She slides the bottle in,
deep as she can,
into the font.

"What have we got here?"
A man's mocking lilt,
resonates from close behind.
Young Sonia turns, red faced and failing
to retain any semblance of composure.

"A-Am I not allowed to take this?"

"Souvenir, is it? You gonna try and
sell it back to us after?"

The man is tall and wiry,
a black shirt and tracksuit bottoms.
Red stubble on his face,
and wiry reddish copper hair.
His unblinking green-grey eyes
and cheesy grin, somehow,
unclean.

"No, my nan—it's just—"

"Are ya gonna try and sell it back
to us after?"

He takes a half step forward.
Sonia freezes where she stands,
confused by the insistent
implication of his words.

"No, I just wanted—"

CROM CRUACH

"After, yeah?"

"Look, I'm not taking any."

Sonia pulls the bottle out,
empties what little that was in it
back into the font,
but this chap, he's closing in
taking another stride toward her.

"After what?" He prompts, expectantly.
Sonia's confused and terrified.
She knows she can't outrun this man.

"Darragh, that's enough."

A middle aged blonde woman
appears out from the church.
Sonia recognises her, she thinks,
from the news,
years and years ago,
when she was just a kid.
"Crazy," the woman was called then.
"Dangerous" and "fascist" too.
A minister or a journalist or something,
back before the war.

Sonia can't recall.
But this man,
Darragh,
ignores the woman.

He screams suddenly at Sonia,
"After you and your jewish faggot
friends burn this place down?!
Yeah?!"

Darragh lunges,
Sonia tries to run,

VALKYRIE LOUGHCREWE

but he manages to grab her arm,
and twists, painfully, until she drops the bottle.
He pushes her away, out of the cathedral.

Retaining balance, she breaks into a sprint,
racing down the winding path,
just as it begins to rain,
her mission failed.

The man picks up the bottle,
pelts Sonia with it as she flees,
and turns to face the angry
woman in the doorway:
Deirdre Ríordáin.

"What have you done?" Deirdre chides.
Darragh punches her.
Breaks her nose,
and she falls backward
to the floor.

Darragh towers over her.

"Get the fuck back inside,
 you worthless fucking cunt."

***

In a wood of oak and ash,
Gearoid sits up in a tree.
Rain buckets down on him,
and he thinks that he can hear
someone calling out his name.

He grasps for his crucifix,
realising to his horror that
he must have lost it off his person.

CROM CRUACH

It's now lying in some mulchy leaves
a small frog hopping past it,
delighting in the rainfall.

Gearoid scrambles from the tree,
and turns to see a figure,
standing there in the overgrowth,
ice blue eyes and mottled flesh.

A hag.

He turns and runs,
afraid the mud will grab his legs,
arrest him from escaping,
but no such horror comes.

Gearoid races to a clearing.
Sonia emerges at the other side.
They stare across the space,
rain pouring down upon them.

They take in the sight of each other's frazzled faces.
Gearoid glances back.

The phantom hag's no longer there.

CHAPTER 7

Marco's pissing amongst the roses,
around the side of the Boyle residence,
feeling conflicted about it, but ultimately,
nature wins over decorum.

The crunch of tires on gravel
confirms his hunch:
The CDA are on the scene.

"They're here!" Iarla calls out, voice cracking.
The poor kid's petrified.

Marco soon sees why,
as he comes around the corner.
There must be ten cars, both in the driveway
and just beyond, parked on the road,
creating a blockade.

The whole damn village showed up.

Against his better nature,
Marco feels panic start to grip his nervous system,
but he steps in front of Iarla.

"Don't worry, lad. I'll handle this."

Yellow vested county council boys,
and a couple of commune's worth
of farmer types, from young to old

CROM CRUACH

all come marching up the driveway,
some armed with bats.

Aaron Larkin, one of those satanists from Breifne,
his head wrapped up in bandages,
due to some explosion at the mechanic's shop,
approaches with a sword.

Marco expects hidden knives,
perhaps a gun or two,
but they're trying to play nice for now.
Mick Rahill, the Trucking Guild
Communications Secretary
takes the lead.

"You were driving around in yer lil cop car this morning?"

"Mrs. Dunne called us this morning,"
Marco speaks calmly, measured,
"said she heard screaming outside."

Iarla's chewing his lip bloody,
his guts like writhing snakes,
he needs to shit,
and puke,
and Mick Rahill speaks aloud again.

"You should have called us,
you're not the police anymore."

"It gives the old ladies
some sense of normalcy,
that's all.
Didn't think it was gonna be anything,
but it was."

Breda Rafferty pipes up from the crowd.

"I'll go check on Mrs. Dunne to clarify."

VALKYRIE LOUGHCREWE

Saoirse Kavanagh steps up, phone in hand.
Another bloody satanist, surely here
to throw the blame on Marco.

"Sure I'll just ring her, sure." she says.

"Just go in there and you'll see.
It's true," Iarla says,
staring down at his feet.

"Is Oisin Hall with you?"
Marco asks.

Oisin emerges from the crowd
looking somehow even worse,
his hair a messy unwashed tangle
from his short nap in some guy's car.

He just stares over at Marco,
and the ex-cop begins to realise,
that he's going to have to say something
about the living dead inside.

"Look, there's a reason we didn't call you lot, "
Marco cringes, his voice cracking.

"—and I don't want to say it out loud,
so just go on and look in there for fuck sake!"

The crack in Marco's voice
is the only trigger Aidan needs.
He strides over from the crowd,
pulling a pistol from his belt.

He shoves it into Marco's face
and grins like a kid at Christmas.

"Shut the fuck up.
Against the wall.

CROM CRUACH

Now,"
Aidan growls.

Marco puts his hands up.

Terry Collier, composed as ever,
her movements, words and tone carefully measured,
places a hand on Aidan's shoulder,
which is immediately shrugged off.

"Maybe put the gun away, man.
Look, I'll go inside and check."

Terry, Jimmy Candon, those bloody pagan bastards,
Hannah Kerrigan, the equestrian—
and one person Marco actually sees as sane—
start moving toward the house,
along with old JohnEd Smith the butcher,
which reassures the ex-cop further,
that some good might get done here today.

Terry lingers at the doorway,
waiting for Aidan to stand down.
He and Marco lock eyes,
frozen sweating enmity.

"You pull that trigger and you're a dead man,"
Mick Rahill gravely states.

Aidan puts the gun in Terry's hand,
and walks back to his car.
Marco exhales his deep relief,
as quietly as he can.

And everyone inside the house
starts screaming at the sight
of something in the living room,
that they will never comprehend.

VALKYRIE LOUGHCREWE

Marco looks over to Oisin,
who meets him with a fearful gaze.
He tries not to have any kind of
I told you so in his face,
and fails.

CROM CRUACH
PART TWO

CHAPTER 8

"*Saint Michael,*
Flaming Sword of God,
Protect her.
Keep those who would harm us away,
and watch over us always.
Amen."

Oisin's dreaming of his altar.
The statue of Saint Michael,
driving his blade into the serpent,
upon a sea of clean white cloth.

Of the prayer he used to say,
and still does to this day,
to keep his lover safe,
wherever she might be.

She'd have protested if she'd known
he'd been putting in a word,
with the divine colonizers,
devout heathen that she was.

That past tense "was" would sting,
if he were awake to let it sit
inside his mind,
but as he sleeps and dreams,
the scene begins to shift
along with his attention,
        to a clearing in the forest,

VALKYRIE LOUGHCREWE

when the sun was warmly shining,
down upon him and lovely Dace,

Hand in hand they walked,
lightly arguing about the merits
of planning an expedition,
to a far flung foreign land
around 15th-century astrology,
as chattering above them,
the crows up in the trees
still carried on their mysterious conversation,
in his dream.

Dace strongly assured him
that the time and place was right
to go and see the world
beyond their small community.

"It's the perfect time to do it,
nothing bad is going to happen."

"What about the journey home?"

"There's another perfect hour.
On the Sunday, I think, two o'clock?
Easy enough to get a ferry
over in that time.
More or less."

"Alright, look, I believe you. "

"But . . . ?" She sighs, expectantly.

"*And* I'll come along."

Dace's face goes blank
then slowly brightens
as the meaning of her lover's
words sinks in.

CROM CRUACH

"Really?
Thank you!
Wait, really?"

"Really.
Life is for living,
isn't it?"

Oisin feels the warmth of her happiness,
and moves in to embrace her,
and wakes up in Terry's car.

They're parked outside the bakery,
that his apartment sits above,
along the main street of the town.

Terry's sitting silently,
shocked at what she saw,
the grisly things inside that house.

Oisin drifts back into dreaming of Dace,
standing in a cloud of incense,
painted aglow with morning light.

"Hey, come on,
don't fall asleep, man."

"Oh God, just let me rest."

"Are you gonna pass out in there
or do I have to go in with you?"

Oisin's expression hardens.
He looks Terry dead in the eye.

"Did you do this?
You . . . the Morrighannain?
Is this . . . one of yours?"

VALKYRIE LOUGHCREWE

Terry's jaw drops,
flummoxed.

"Are you sa—
are you asking if
we *killed the Boyles?*"

"I'm not asking that,
I'm asking . . .
The fact that they're still moving around
doesn't fit with any of
your recent rituals or . . . ?"

"Man, are you kidding me?
We're not fucking *necromancers.*
Well . . . we are, technically, but—
like—
this shit doesn't happen.
It doesn't happen.
And if we're being totally honest with each other
I don't know if your little Jesus toys
are gonna do anything about it."

"You think *you* guys could stop it?"

"If we figure out where it's coming from, yeah.
But you're the Catholic, exorcism is kinda your thing.
And I doubt they're gonna let us in there to do *our* thing,
so you may as well try.
You've never even heard of anything like this before,
from the Franciscans?"

"Only in folklore, and even then, it's nothing major. "

"Can you remember *what?*"

Oisin shakes his head.

CROM CRUACH

"Like generic, revenant type things
coming back due to unfinished business
in Celtic lore? I'm not sure if I remember it properly.
I can get in contact with the brotherhood,
and—"

Terry shakes her head.

"I don't want monks down here.
I don't want the church involved.
We've fought so fucking hard
to get their fingers out of this community.
No offence."

"Fuck you" Oisin sighs.
He opens the door,
pulling his exhausted frame
out into the street.

"Oisin. We're all on the same side, okay?"

Oisin turns back to face her.
He tries to look hardened but
finds himself just so exhausted,
on the verge of tears.

"Why did Dace leave?" he asks, point blank.

Terry pauses,
trying to gather her thoughts.

"I don't know."

"Have you talked to her?"

"You know I haven't, man, c'mon."

Oisin drags his aching heavy form,
around the back of McDonnell's bakery,

VALKYRIE LOUGHCREWE

so as to not offend the senses
of those customers
expecting the sweet smell of baking bread,
and not the smell of unwashed sessioner
with an unsightly case of bedhead.

Oisin trudges up the stairwell,
and leans against the door.
He shoves his face into his arm,
sheds a silent stream of tears,
before turning to face his duty.

His apartment is in chaos
piles of books and clothes,
fast food containers.
He's been sleeping on the couch
since she disappeared.

He searches for the materials
that he requires for the exorcism.
Grunting with exhaustion and frustration
at his lack of organisational skills.

Incense, censer, crucifix,
statue of the archangel,
a grimoire, *Hygromanteia*.
He keeps dropping things and
losing track.
His brain is fried.
This day fucking sucks.

His bedroom is a bombsite.
Misplaced miscellania,
all strewn across the bed.
He spies the last thing that he needs:
a small box of frankincense
crushed underneath a heavy book.

"Alright."

CROM CRUACH

He sighs and grabs it up,
when a sound explodes behind him,
from the doorway,
ear splitting cawing—
he whirls around in fright to see.

A crow? In the apartment?

Standing in the open door,
clothed in ragged shadows,
will-o-wisp blue burning lights,
glowing inside her empty sockets.

A mottled, grey, bog-body hag,
toothless shrivelled mouth agape.
an elongated corvid clicking,
emitting from her mossy throat.

He feels a slimy squirming,
coming from between his fingers
so he looks down at his hands,
they're caked in sodden, wormy earth.

The creatures writhe across his palms,
they burrow into apertures,
opening up across his skin.

arís anseo . . .
tiocfaidh gort . . .

"You need a hand with that?
 Maybe get a bag?"

Everything is white,
the sun shining in his eyes,
Oisin's standing on the footpath by the car,
barely managing to carry
all of the objects that he needs
to perform the exorcism.

VALKYRIE LOUGHCREWE

He looks around confused,
crows circling above the townhouses,
and scavenging down on the road.
Wasn't he just inside . . . ?

"Is this . . . "

"Oisin? Hello?" Terry waves at him, concerned.

"Are—are you threatening me?" Oisin asks her.

Terry looks taken aback,
laughs nervously.

"What?"

"What the hell was that, Terry?"

Terry steps forward, cautiously,
helps take some of the load
out of Oisin's arms.

"Oisin, man, you're talking shite,
dude, we need you to focus up?"

Oisin just sits down, then
in the middle of the footpath
clutching incense, book,
statue, censer,
mind spinning with confusion.

"Fuck,
you do need some sleep, don't you.
Get into the back seat.
I'll take the long way round."

CHAPTER 9

Most of the folks who were present
at the Boyles' house have gone home.
Those who still remain on shift are fully armed
wth rifles, shotguns and the like.

The road blockade is gone,
but a perimeter is set,
no one enters or gets out,
without the Community Defence Alliance
knowing all about it.

Around the back, sat on the doorstep,
Aaron with the bandaged head
and Leanne Conaty, another Morrighannain member
share in a tense smoke.

In the presence of James Tackney,
a farmer they don't know well,
beyond the times they've traded cattle
and machinery and the like.

They've been chatting small talk,
mainly business
How's the farm? Grand!
How is yours?
Leanne I hear you've been making soaps!
I have!
and on and on and on.

CROM CRUACH

A lot is being left unsaid,
between the two occultists.
The sound of tires on gravel,
interrupts an awkward lull.

"That'd be them, so," James bluntly states.

He heads round the corner.
Leanne and Aaron hang behind,
relieved to finally be able
to freely speak their minds.

"We should be recording this.
Getting evidence," Leanne says.

"No. No. Those are our neighbours,"
Aaron warns.

"Those are physical manifestations
of paranormal phenomenon the likes
of which nobody has ever seen in
hundreds of years, maybe ever. It's
our duty—"

"It's our duty to keep the community
safe, healthy, happy, and most
important, okay with us doing what we
do. This'd be pushing it, to say the
least. We're probably already
the main suspects here."

Leanne takes an angry, ragged breath,
and throws away her smoke.

"History is just going to keep
repeating itself, isn't it?"

Sitting patiently in the living room,
with wreckage all around him,

VALKYRIE LOUGHCREWE

shattered porcelain, sour milk
and a splintered kitchen table,

Padraig Boyle's eyeless revenant.
Bound to the couch by christmas lights,
staring sightlessly. And tied up next to him,
the undead shade of Lynda.

Iarla had the courtesy to drape a blanket over her,
covering the obscene remains of what used to be her head.
The blood far too coagulated at that point to soak through linen,
almost looking like a child dressed as a ghost, playing pretend.

She'd look almost alive if it wasn't so glaringly apparent,
how much of her skull is missing,
a chasm where there should be a rounded dome.

The telly's on, flat blue dead channel
and they're breathing like they never died,
as Oisin lights the censer
and prepares to cleanse the home.

James Tackney and Jimmy Candon,
sprinkle holy water on the second floor,
billowing clouds of frankincense,
arising all throughout the house.

Oisin shuts his eyes,
recites a prayer to God's hand, Michael
and hopes that what he's got arranged
can really drive this weirdness out.

As the frankincense scent reaches
Padraig's revenant, he sniffs,
and a deep guttural hum,
starts to vibrate within his throat.

Lynda starts a wheezy rasping,
somewhat muffled beneath her shroud,

CROM CRUACH

as her shattered head attempts
to match and harmonise with Padraig.

The exorcist's words falter,
as he hears the corpses humming,
but he finishes the first,
of his prayer's repetition,
and then calls out to the bodies.

"Hello? Can you hear me? Can you
answer me?"

He approaches the two bodies,
they do not seem to be responsive,
So he points his ritual dagger,
and repeats.

The latin prayer
to the archangel

"Mi! Cha! El!"

He bellows piously,
and the corpses of the Boyles,
erupt fully into song.

The voices pouring from their throats
high pitched, childlike, echoing
Oisin's prayer back at him like a chorus.
He stops, consumed by fear,
adrenaline overpowering his tired brain.

Lynda's shade starts to strain
against her bonds.
They creak
They snap.

Oisin looks around but
it seems that he's alone.

VALKYRIE LOUGHCREWE

He wants to scream for help
but chokes on fear.

Lynda wriggles free, rises
from the couch. She steps toward him,
grasping blindly,
though not as blindly as he'd want.

Sheet slips away,
reveals the true extent
of her fatal mutilation
a bloody, broken lower jaw,
the rest of her head missing,
and an undulating tongue,
half torn out at the stem.

Black blood bubbling from ruptured muscle
as she sings.

Padraig bursts forth from his bonds,
as Lynda's undead shade lunges forward,
pinning Oisin against the mantlepiece
with swift and unexpected force.

The sharp angled polished wood,
shoves against his ribs so violently.
Where has everybody gone!?
I need help, why can't I scream!?

She pins him there and holds him,
With inhuman strength, as Padraig
takes the fire iron up,
raises it above his head.

And from the deepest,
blood clogged recess,
of her shattered, exposed trachea
In a childlike, morbid gurgle
Lynda says,

CROM CRUACH

"Be . . .
Not . . .
Afraid"

James Tackney tackles Padraig,
into the wreckage of the table,
Nails and splinters pierce the both of them
as they wrestle in the debris.

Lynda takes Oisin by the hair,
slams his head into the mantlepiece
all goes white for him, mind spinning.
She pulls back his head again.

Before she can subject him
to another vicious impact
Leanne and Aaron, Mick and Terry
pull her off of him, he goes stumbling
and trips over the couch.

Saoirse pulls him to his feet and drags him
out into the hall, through the porch
into the garden, where the fresh air
stirs his senses, from numb dizziness to pain.

Jimmy races in from out the back
the room filling with a roar
as the chainsaw goes to work
making sure the problem's fixed.

Saoirse, waiting on a medkit,
to deal with Oisin's bloody head wound,
on the front step of the Boyle's house,
checks him for concussion.

"W-what's going on in there?"
He asks about the racket from inside.

VALKYRIE LOUGHCREWE

Without missing a beat
Saoirse replies to him,

"Plan B."

CHAPTER 10

The forest
seems eternal.

A thousand acres,
so forgotten by the world
that it was never even classified
as wilderness.

Getting this deep into the woods
before the sun goes down completely,
was never going to be any kind of
safe or easy journey.

They prepared themselves for failure
Saoirse, Goran, and Jimmy
with enough supplies for morning,
and they indeed did end up failing,

So they approach the site in darkness,
crouched, almost crawling through thick brush.
Sweating, tired, fearing the trek back to the cars.

Their flashlights pick up only insects,
brambles and long grass.
Maybe they've forgotten where they left it.
Maybe they've ventured out too far.

Then emerging from the darkness,
a yellowed shroud all tangled up,

suspended in the thorny branches,
like a child's drawing of a ghost.

Torn and cast aside
above a hole dug in the earth
exhumed and ruined
six foot deep
and two foot wide.

"Who squealed?" Jimmy asks.

"I don't think anybody would have."
Goran replies,
looking around in fear,
of who or what
may have set this
as a trap.

"Too much to lose," he whispers.

"She didn't crawl out of there herself, man!" Jimmy's panicking.

"Are you so sure of that?" Saoirse asks.

"Cause I'm fuckin' not. Not anymore."

***

Gearoid Boyle is hiding, best he can,
pressed up against a bush,
at the side of a back road.
A car drives past

He's dressed in black,
trying to blend in with the shadows.
He isn't sure if they saw him,
but they don't stop,
and that's good enough.

CROM CRUACH

He keeps on walking
down the road which winds darkly
toward Sonia's,
where she said that she'd be waiting,
with their other friends from school.

He's going to tell them everything
though it could be putting them in danger.
He can't face this shit alone,
or he's going to lose his mind.

The house sits on a hill
at a crossroads, above a bog.
Groundwater's always causing ruptures
in the tarmac, forming potholes,
at a relentless rate of entropy.

If it weren't for the councilmen,
regularly coming by to patch things up,
that old dark house would rot there,
isolated, on an island hill.

As he trudges up the incline,
toward the Kavanagh family house,
He thinks on old man Fintan,
that reeking, trembling spectre.

Gearoid saw him once without
the leather gloves he always wears,
his shaking fingers gnarled, the nails removed.
Sonia told him that was from back during the war
when his fellow landlords,
punished him for siding with his daughter.

Sonia meets him at the door
Dressed oddly formally,
looking nervous.
Gearoid cold and wet, bedraggled,
just wants to get in from the rain.

VALKYRIE LOUGHCREWE

"Come on," she says.
"Let's deal with this."

She takes the lad's cold hand,
and leads him through the hall.
The warmth offers little comfort,
for the chill in him is deep

"Where are the others?" He asks.

"They're just in here."

She leads him to the living room, a fire lit,
and sitting there is Fintan,
nursing another glass of whiskey.

"No."
Gearoid erupts, and tries to flee,
but Sonia grips him.

"Gearoid—Gearoid—this is the right
thing to do."

"You lied to me."

Fintan motions to an old armchair across from him.

"Sit down there, son. Go on. You're
safe now."

Gearoid's adrenaline is coursing,
fight or flight, he won't let himself let go,
let his mind quiet,
and feel,
and feel,
his parents—

CROM CRUACH

Sonia gets in front of him,
she meets his squirming gaze

"It's going to be alright. Whatever it is, we'll
deal with it."

He focuses his mind away,
from what might cause him tears,
to the immediate situation,
the danger, and the need to flee.

He lets himself move forward,
and sit across from Fintan.

Help might be an option.
Then again, if he's mistaken . . .

"You don't understand," he starts, shakily.
"I think you're in danger being around me."

Fintan regards him quietly,
with steely grey
bloodshot eyes,
then speaks.

"Do you owe money to someone, is
that it? Who did you piss off?"

"It's not like that. It's . . . "
Gearoid squirms around in his chair,
looking around for an exit.

"Can't you just forget you ever saw me?"

"Who did it, son? Who killed them?"

"I don't know. I couldn't see him.
He was dark . . . N-not like that.
It was like . . . like a shadow. I . . .

I was watching everything like . . .
Like I was floating. Above the house.
Looking down through the ceiling.
And the house was . . . It was surrounded
By . . . "

He chokes on his next words,
unable to find an appropriate description,
of the things that ringed his house.
The people standing in the trees,
their eyes glowing like embers.
The slither of the creatures in the grass,
like slugs lifting their heads,
and sheep sliced open, gutted,
no heads, just legs and haunches,
orifices sputtering, and among these creatures,
standing, watching;

"I saw my granddad Pat there. He was
crying. And then I was outside, and
running, and I could feel them still,
around me. Mocking me."

"Who?" Fintan asked. "Who was around you?"

"That wasn't even the start of it,
for weeks before this . . .
I'd been having these
dreams, and things in the house
kept . . . Being moved around and—
Look, I think being around me is
putting you in danger.
I think I'm haunted or something.
Cursed."

"You're in shock."
Fintan laments, shaking his head.

CROM CRUACH

"Look you've got to tell me,
if you saw who did it.
We've got to catch the bastard.
Have you had any dealings with my daughter,
Saoirse? Or her friends?
You can tell me if this has something to do with them."

"It was a shadow. A *shadow*.
I'm not sure that it was even a person."

The trio in the living room,
so attentive as they are,
to each others micro-movements,
every word and facial expression,
that they don't notice the fire streaking,
toward the windowpane.

The flaming molotov,
breaks through the glass,
coming as a visceral shock.

It erupts in spreading flames,
devouring the curtains,
spilling across the table.
Gearoid and Fintan spring up.

"I'm sorry!" Gearoid wails
and bolts for the front door.

"It's not safe out there!" Fintan cries.
"Sonia, go up to the attic and hide!
I'll get the gun."

"I'm calling Saoirse," Sonia declares.

"Yes, good, just go!"

Gearoid throws the front door open.
There are men out on the driveway.

VALKYRIE LOUGHCREWE

Feral shadows under moonlight,
with the heads of wolves, animal skins,
draped over their own
and beneath that, all black clothing.
Balaclavas hide their faces.

Sonia grabs his shoulder
"Come hide! We can—"

An arrow from the darkness
pierces through her shoulder.

She shrieks and staggers backward,
grips the wall to keep from falling.
The men on the driveway
start toward the house.

Back in the garage,
Fintan turns the key and pops the lock
on the rifle case and loads it in a hurry.

His drink-clouded mind is spinning;
stop the intruders, douse the fire,
before everything I know and love
is taken once again.

He stands up to turn,
to fight.
The power cuts,
the light goes out.

There's a shadow in the corner,
with a long dark coat and wide brimmed hat,
that wasn't there before.

Fintan screams, raises to fire,
but the shadow's just too fast.

CROM CRUACH

Gearoid, frozen, stares as Sonia
is blocked out from his sight,
by the men in wolfskin.

They rush the house, race right past him,
knives out, raised and darkly eager.

Even if he had the will left,
wasn't broken by despair
a pair of black-gloved hands apprehend him,
hold him still.
He shuts his eyes as their daggers plunge,
and his friend cries out her last.

They pull Gearoid away,
throw him roughly from the house.
He falls hard, but they don't let him rest.
They turn him around to look into
the fire and the darkness.

Lit through his bleary tears,
the flames conjure the perfect glamour,
that these really aren't men,
but savage beasts
with the heads of wolves.

"Run along now, little deer.
Go, find help, tell them, we dare you.
You know how this is going to end."

CHAPTER 11

Fay's pub is the place
where the older crowd frequent,
controversial in staying open
all day, all night, all week
with little exception.

There's always somebody around,
to keep things good and civil.
The air is full of smoke, and rebel songs,
old and new, drunken chatter,
and the clattering of the pool table.

A red haired woman by the name of Robin,
smirks as Marco misses his shot,
the cueball clacking into two of hers.

"You're getting rusty, old man," she says.

"Gold doesn't rust, my dear," Marco responds.

"Well that's two to me, Mr. Gold."

"You threw me off."

"All part of the game, right?"

He takes a swig of whiskey,
as he watches Robin lining up her shot.
A wiry looking fella with a weathered, gaunt complexion,
plops a watch down at the table.

CROM CRUACH

"I'll play the winner, yeah?"

"You will in your arse, man," Marco grunts.
"Piss off."

"That's not very nice, Sarge," Robin says,
repositioning, overthinking the shot, Marco reckons.

"I'll play you, darling. For me earrings," she tells the newcomer.

The guy who bet his watch side-eyes Marco,
afraid to meet his gaze.
He asks,

"Is it true you were down at the Boyle's House?"

Robin goes for it,
the cueball ricochets once, twice,
the trick shot lands, she pots a double.

"Who wants to know?
Nice shot, Robin."

"Padraig was my best friend, man.
He ran Dungeons & Dragons
for me and the wee lad."

"You're shittin' me," Marco scoffs.

"I'm serious.
I can't bring myself to tell wee Jack
that we'll never find out
if that cat is the real king
of the fae court or not . . .
He's on the spectrum,
and it was a routine, you know?"

"Oh, that's so awful," Robin earnestly laments.

VALKYRIE LOUGHCREWE

"What's awful," Marco grumbles,
"is that we're letting the satanists that killed them
walk all over this community."

"Satanists?"
The man looks taken aback.

Marco puts down his drink and erupts,
addressing the entire pub.

"The whole family was butchered in an occult ritual,
carried out by the church burning
pagans up in Breifne!"

The entire pub, in this instance,
includes Jimmy Candon, sitting at the bar,
nursing a pint and tugging on
a thick blunt that's been going around.

A chill runs up his spine,
and his cheeks flush hot with anger,
but he takes a long, deep breath.
He's used to this sort of thing.

"We were warned, over and over again,
before we let children with guns
change how this country was run.
Witchcraft, black magic.
Now they're killing families.
and they're gonna kill more!"

A couple of aul boys raise their glasses and roar assent.
Jimmy stands up, as a couple of his townie mates
try and hold him back.

"It's not worth it," they murmur
but he speaks up.

CROM CRUACH

"What the fuck are you saying man?"
He calls out to the ex-Garda.

Marco rolls his eyes.

"Oh, Jesus Christ, here's one of them now.
What are you going to do, knacker?
Fight me?"

"Nah man. You're just standing here lying.
We were all up sessioning at the gaff last night.
Ask Fionnuala Smith or Gerry McEvoy or anyone.
We weren't burning churches or killing kids or any of that shite,
     Marco.
Cop on."

A couple of the auld boys rise to back up Marco.
Stanley Redmond, Fergus Foxall, two lads rumored to have been
allied with the fascists, but survived the war on just enough
     accounts,
of people claiming "ahh they're sound".

"I think you'd better leave, Jimmy,"
Fergus smiles at him,
changing the grip on his beer bottle,
from recreational to offensive

"Hey, what's this shit?" Robin asks the boys. "Don't be startin'
     fights in here."
"Where's the barman?" someone shouts
and sure enough no barkeep can be seen.

"I don't wanna fight, Marco," Jimmy sighs.
"I'm just having a jar before I tip off home."

"You gonna just let him accuse you of murdering kids like that?"
Tony, Jimmy's cousin asks him
calling from across the pub.

VALKYRIE LOUGHCREWE

"I'm not even of a mind to pay heed to such shite, look at him,
     he's pathetic."

Marco growls, grabs the cue from Robin's hands and moves
     toward Jimmy.
Fergus breaks his bottle, Stanley fishes in his pocket for his brass
     knuckles.

"ALRIGHT EVERYBODY COOL IT NOW. "

Tonights beleaguered barkeeper,
a chap named SungWon Hak,
has emerged from the back room,
armed with a twelve gauge shotgun,

"I am not afraid to paint the walls with any of you cunts. Alright?
 So Marco, Jimmy, get the fuck out.
 Marco out the back, Jimmy out the front. "

"Yeah SungWon, right, yeah,"
Jimmy says, raising his arms and walking toward the door
"Nice one, I'm off."

Marco shoves the pool cue
into the hands of the wiry gaunt man,
who didn't expect when he left the house,
to hear tall tales of devil worship.

"Have fun losing your watch, nerd."

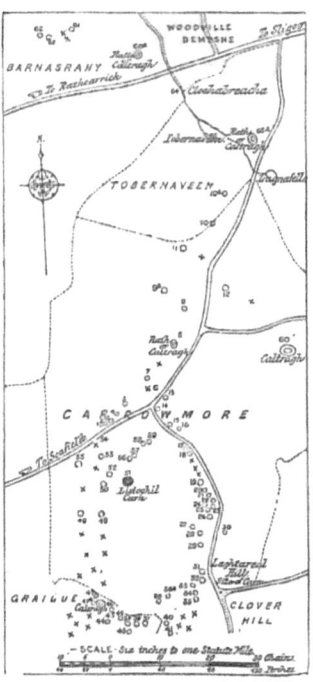

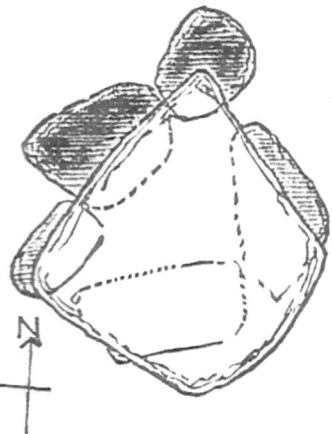

County Sligo, just west of Cavan County, is home to one of the oldest and largest megalithic sites to be found in all of Ireland.

Today, the Carrowmore Megalithic Cemetery is comprised of thirty individual stone tombs, dating back as far as 3700 B.C.

But it is unknown how many more tombs might have made up the original Carrowmore complex throughout *(cont'd.)*

CHAPTER 12

Oisin lies in bed unsure,
if he's sleeping or awake.
There's an apparition
standing at the foot of his bed.
A chieftain holding in both hands
a shining, bleeding sword.
The crimson ichor flows,
from his calloused fingers,
running down the blade
his steel eyes shimmering with tears.

Oisin can't speak,
can't ask him,
Who are you?

He thinks,
trying to send the words across the room,
his inner voice sounding like
a drowning child inside him.

A pair of pale, bare arms,
slide around the chieftain's shoulders.
From behind him hangs a figure.
Her pale face slinks around,
black pits for eyes,
serenely smiling.

Dace has come back home.

CROM CRUACH

Oisin wakes up,
feeling nauseous.
It's still dark,
and his room still reeks,
of all the things he should have put away,
by this point in his grieving.

He wants to go get some food,
or drink something; coffee, whiskey, anything.
He wants a smoke, to go for a walk.
Anything but to sleep again.

He knows his next dreams will be more restful.
It will be morning before he knows it.
As distressing as that last dream was,
He wants it to stay the last dream that he had
to be able to say it was.

He feels like she's still here.
He wants to see her once again,
maybe huddled in the corner of his room,
like some sleep paralysis demon.

Oisin drifts back to sleep.

***

Some hours later he finds himself
sipping tea on a recliner, in a greenhouse,
filled with cannabis,
as Podge and his wife Mannion,
tend their crop, and music drifts over the radio.

"I wouldn't be surprised.
That's how it always goes in the films,"
Podge responds,
to something Oisin said,
about the local pagans,
and what their practice may have wrought.

VALKYRIE LOUGHCREWE

"This kind of thing just doesn't really happen in real life though,"
Oisin ponders.

"No? I always assumed you'd be out
dealing with mad shit like that
with the monks. "

"Really? I never got the sense that you were a believer,"
Oisin says.

"Hmm. I suppose not really, come to think of it.
I never did think about it enough to believe or not believe.
You were just out doing your thing.
I've never really cared enough to have, like,
an opinion on supernatural stuff other than,
'I dunno'."

"How has this not come up before?"
Mannion scoffs.

"Too much going on," Podge says.

"But you two, like, hang out all the time."

"Maybe I'm his refuge from all that shit. Whaddaya think, Ois?"

Oisin's not paying attention.
He says,
"It's got to have something to do with
the church burnings, right?
Maybe it's . . . angry Catholics.
Fascists."

"That doesn't explain the
zombies though, does it?"
Podge says,
lighting up a spliff,
and passing it to his wife.

CROM CRUACH

"Maybe—that's just a random thing,"
Oisin postulates.
"Maybe we're being absolute fools
focusing on that whole thing
instead of getting forensics,
looking for a killer."

"Nobody got forensics?"
Mannion asks, concerned.

"I don't know. I hope so.
But how much can you
learn from bodies
that attack you when you get near them? "

"Good point," Podge says.

"I knew a chap back in the day,"
Mannion begins,
"Ryan Shields, he was working on this . . .
death metal album
based on folklore from around here."

"Was it any good?"

"Oh, it was shite. Guitars sounded like muck,
vocals were too loud and just laughable,
and the drums were the same looped beat
pulled from a, like, youtube drum tutorial.
Couldn't have sounded worse if he tried.
And I think he tried, to be honest. "

"Does anyone want tea?"
Oisin asks.
"I'm going to make more."

"Don't interrupt me," Mannion chides.

VALKYRIE LOUGHCREWE

"Sorry."

"I do want tea though." She says with a wink.

Oisin opens his mouth,
to say something smarmy,
but decides wisely against it.
Mannion continues.

"It was about, like, this place—Cavan.
Apparently this is where,
in the medieval times or whatever,
they used to sacrifice babies to an evil god
Crom. Like in *Conan*?
But in the folklore he's like a big . . .
worm or something. Or a snake. "

Oisin recalls a strange memory,
worms crawling on his hands, *inside* his hands.

He recalls the strangeness of being inside,
and then outside, after a vision of . . . something.
Something in his room.

He can't quite recall—how could he have forgotten?
It's like a dream.
This could be something.
He leans forward, riveted.

"Is that right?" He prompts her to continue.

"Yeah, the whole county used to have this other name.
Macnas, or something.
That cathedral up there, Saint Patrick's?
That's the exact spot where Saint Pat himself defeated Crom,
and drove the pagans out or whatever it is."

"Are you shitting me?" Oisin exclaims.
That *is* something.

CROM CRUACH

"How did you not know that, Oisin?"
Podge chuckles.

"Did *you* know that, Podge?"
He shoots back.

"No, but I don't know anything."

"You said to me before Ois," Mannion says,
"that the entire Catholic faith is one great
big exorcism of evil spirits, right?
Well, what if the church burnings
are bringing them back?"

"Looking for babies to eat?" Podge laughs.

"Why not?"

Oisin is up
pacing now, trying to think.
Too much noise in his brain.
Crom.
Killycluggin.
Macnas? No, that can't be right.
That's a parade they have in Galway or something,
or a theatre company from around there.

"This makes too much sense.
I'm trying not to jump to conclusions here. But Dace.
She wouldn't. She wouldn't want anything to do with that kind of
    thi—"

His blood runs cold.

"Maybe that's why she left?" Podge suggests

"Maybe she didn't leave," Oisin intones, gravely.

VALKYRIE LOUGHCREWE

Mannion, the voice of reason, chimes in.

"I've known Leanne and Goran since I was in school.
They're weird, and they fuck around with demonology and shit,
I know that. But they're good people.
They're not baby killers and they sure wouldn't slaughter a whole
    family.
So maybe narrow it down a bit more before getting the angry
    mob together."

"You're right, I am jumping to conclusions. I'm just . . . this is a
    lot. "

"Have we ruled out the pigs?" Podge asks, expelling a gout of
    weed smoke.

"Pigs?"

"Well, ex-pigs."

"Ah yeah. Anything's possible, but why would they go after
    Dace?"

"She probably just left, man."

Oisin flushes.
The idea of Dace being dead was rough,
but the idea that she just
left him is somehow even worse,
and he hates himself for that.

"I gotta go," he says,
setting down the empty teacup,
he had been fondling nervously.

"Man, stick around, chill out, smoke some weed."
 Podge offers the boof.

CROM CRUACH

"I need some air, man, I'm sorry."
Oisin leaves at speed, rattled.
Mannion shoots Podge a dirty look.
He shrugs at her;

"What?"

CHAPTER 13

The Morrighannain are all gathered
in the commune farmhouse,
all around a table,
where there rests a deck of cards.

Cora's feeling out of place,
on the arm of Saoirse's chair.
Not officially a member,
of their little club quite yet,
so they're clearly holding back.

She can tell that there are words
being left unsaid, phrases coded,
due to her unwanted presence.
Though Saoirse said that she was welcome,
Cora can feel that this is not the case.

Terry Collier's in the centre,
of the big old antique couch.
On either side sit Goran and Leanne,
and Aidan stands behind them
smoking.

Aaron sits across from Saoirse
the opposing end of the table,
and the house's ginger cat,
named Fortune,
lies in a patch of sunshine,
snoozing sweetly.

CROM CRUACH

Cora wonders for the first time
if an accident at the garage
is what really happened to Aaron's face.
She's growing painfully aware
of how little she knows about these people,
and the weird shit that they practice,
in the dark where no one's watching,
in the places no one goes.

She glances toward Jimmy, who is standing by the window,
staring out at the springtime sunshine, his facial features grim.
She wonders why such a practical sort of mincéir,
so different from these hipsters,
is involved so damn intensely
in the nonsense they espouse.

Am I just bitter because they haven't let me join them?
Am I just sore because I couldn't possibly relate,
to the bond they all must share
from fighting together in the war?

I hid myself away, I fled.
I waited out the violence
In Cuba, safe as houses.
I physically couldn't—
So I told myself.
Just starting HRT, afraid
of being queer in wartime
what might happen—
God I'm so ashamed.
Saoirse says she doesn't care.
None of them have ever judged me
So they say,
my chest is getting tight and the air is getting heavy.
Maybe i should step outside

"What are you doing? You're thinking too big.
We just need to figure out where she is,"

VALKYRIE LOUGHCREWE

Leanne says, leaning over Terry's tarot spread.

Terry grunts in irritation, continuing her work,
trying to expend as little mental energy,
debating divinatory etiquette as she can.

Jimmy pleads Leanne to back off,
to let the woman work.
Stepping away from the window
he crouches at the table's edge
as Terry flips the first card:

Judgement

"Here's our killer," Terry exhales.

"Who is it?" Cora asks.

"It's not a who, it's more a what,"
 Aaron chimes in meekly.

"Court cards,
Kings, Queens,
y'know,
are people.
Major Arcana, trumps.
They're cosmic forces,
bigger than any of us."

Heat rushes to Cora's face, embarrassed,
to be here, to be hearing this.
Cosmic forces? People are dying and someone's to blame.
Not some abstract force.
But she holds her tongue.

Terry flips the next—*the Two of Cups*—
and the next.
The King of Coins.
The killer dining with a figure of wealth.

CROM CRUACH

A dispute on wealth's true meaning
briefly sparks among the pagans
but is doused by Terry's
loud announcement of the next card:
The Hanged Man.

"Oh, I'm sorry," Leanne protests, indignantly.
"Did you not want us to try and figure this out togeth—"

"THIS CARD," Terry begins,
 forcefully enough to throw Leanne off her protest,
"is us. Suspended, confused, trying to receive wisdom."

"Bit on the nose. Not very helpful," Aaron says.

"But it is accurate," Jimmy notes. "So maybe it's right about the
     killer too."

"I thought trump cards were supposed to be cosmic forces, not
     people," Goran suggests.

He is left ignored.

The smell of incense is starting
to give Cora a headache,
She wants to step outside
let this ephemeral bickering
burn itself out.

Terry reluctantly lays down two more cards,
spurred on to violate her traditional Crowleyian spread
by those insisting that it's not a crime to break
some stodgy dead man's rules.
She turns them over:
The Chariot
and
Princess of Swords.

VALKYRIE LOUGHCREWE

"A young scientist?" Terry sighs. "A studious . . . girl?"

"No, no. That's not right," Saoirse says.
"Look at the way she's facing.
She's facing the chariot,
facing The Hanged Man,
facing us."

"So something's coming our way," Aidan says through gritted
     teeth,
and a chill runs down Cora's spine.

A loud knock on the door then,
turning all heads.

Another knock,
a slow and steady
rapping at the door,
causing them to jump,
like frightened deer.

Aidan rushes to the window.
Whoever it is must be standing there,
right up against the front door,
inside the porch, the angle's bad.

"I can't see shit," he grunts.

"I'll get my gun,"
Saoirse bolts toward the stairs.

"Fuck this," says Aidan gruffly.
He pushes the window open
and hops out onto the gravel.

Cora sits staring,
across the old cottage living room,
as Saoirse's footsteps rush upstairs.
Everyone else gets up and moves,

toward the front door, or the window,
panicking.

Cora just stares over at the wallpaper,
floral, quaint and ancient.
Though the rough arm of the empty chair
has begun to numb her legs,
she doesn't move.

How many people lived here before them
who would consider them *evil*?
And how many of them dreamed,
in secret,
of living lives like theirs?

Aidan screams outside.
A ragged shout of primal terror
and Cora shuts her eyes,
forces herself to remember,
when she came here for the first time.

Stepping through the threshold,
allowing herself to feel hopeful,
to lose the fear,
which had defined her
for the majority of her life.

It's getting hard to breathe
hard to ignore the people screaming
rushing out into the garden
Wait—
did one of them just say

Sonia?

***

Saoirse's mouth tastes metallic.
She bursts into her room and

VALKYRIE LOUGHCREWE

hears Aidan scream outside.
Her room reeks of unwashed clothes
and bedsheets left too long unchanged.

She picks up her rifle, loads it,
heart is racing, mind shot through
with fragmentary prayers and mantras for protection.

Part of her considering just
ducking out the back and running for it.
But a scent memory, somehow,
carries for a moment,
through the stale smell of the bedroom,
of the main street of Cavan town.

Where they ambushed from the windows,
cut down a marching fash procession,
Who were oh so smugly declarative,
of their dominance of the area.

How they shot those fuckers down.
A definitive, *"no you fucking do not."*
Must be a smell off of the rifle
bringing back that distant memory.

She's stopped halfway down the staircase,
by Jimmy, pale and shaken.

"You don't wanna see this, wait a bit."

She frowns and pushes past him,
as something cold and heavy,
starts to claim her from within.

Limbs first, buzzing
creeping weakness
Beckoning her to buckle down and
lie still, flat on the floor.
Some oppressive intuition.

CROM CRUACH

They're gathering in the garden
around something.
Groaning, wordless,
frightened animals attempting,
to deal with something beyond their
frame of reference.

She keeps a hold on her gun,
though it's clear that,
whatever it is,
it isn't threatening her comrades.

Others try to stop her,
her specifically.
She struggles through, now angry.

"What the fuck is going on?"

Standing in the middle of the crowd,
her sister

Sonia.

Ashen skin,
dressed in her formal clothes
all torn, stained black with blood
from a thousand stab wounds.
Lower jaw gone.
Ears removed.

Her dead eyes lock on Saoirse's,
and that buzzing weakness,
detonates like fireworks,
out from her limbs to heart and head,
and Saoirse falls on hands and knees.

A primal scream from somewhere deeper
than her conscious mind erupts.

VALKYRIE LOUGHCREWE

Sustained, throat shredding
keening wail.

She doesn't hear the others call out,
or Sonia's footsteps shuffling near.
She feels the steel plunge through her neck
just above the shoulderblade.

The others tackle back the revenant,
and wrestle away the knife,
it had been concealing,
from their sight.

They pull Saoirse up,
and carry her back toward the house.
The last she sees of her sister is
a jawless, slavering ghoul,
being dragged off by her accomplices
away out to the barn.

CHAPTER 14

A bull's haunch twitches,
sends a scatter of flies spiralling
just far enough away for the creature's comfort
before landing again, on its warm, shit caked fur.

The beast groans as it chews the grass,
idly staring through the fence,
at three strange apes dragging something
struggling against their grasp.

To the bull it seems like a writhing mound
of shit, for the ground to take
and convert back into food.
But to Goran, Leanne and Aidan,
the jawless thing is still called Sonia,
and she's strong, wearing them out.

Leanne throws her full weight
down upon the revenant,
which stands a full head shorter than her.
She knocks it to the muddy ground.

"Lads, just break her limbs!" She cries.
"We can't make it like this."

"Oh Christ, help us," Goran shrieks,
and the revenant makes this
repetitive clicking noise.
It almost sounds like laughter.

VALKYRIE LOUGHCREWE

Goran at first staggers back,
the thought of
just
snapping someone's limbs like that
overwhelming,
causing his gorge to rise.

He feels the vomit rush upwards through his
nostrils and out his mouth.

Aidan throws himself into the task.
He isolates one flailing arm,
leverages it with his leg,
to pull and snap,
surprisingly loud,
almost like a rifle shot.

Goran looks around to see
if anyone is watching,
if anybody knows.

But it's just them,
the dirt road,
the cows in the fields on either side,
and the crows circling above,
in the big grey sky.

Back over at the house
they have Saoirse on the couch.
She sobs uncontrollably
as Cora and Jimmy each put pressure on the stab wound.

"Just let me die,
Let me die
It was supposed to be over
We won
We WON!"

"It's gonna be okay baby, okay?"

CROM CRUACH

Cora's saying words she doesn't believe.
Playing a role in a scene from a horror film.

When did she stop being herself and become this
character in someone else's story?
One she doesn't even understand?

"It's not okay!"

Of course it's not Saoirse, play along for fuck's sake
please, for me.

"And it WAS over!
WE WON!
And we had to go pull that THING
into the world like IDIOTS!"

Cora's blood runs cold,
You mother fuckers
she screams in her head,
You CAUSED THIS
but she fucking holds her stupid, idiot
tongue again.

Bandage-faced Aaron brings the medkit into the room,
his shaking hands
barely keeping grip.

"We gotta get a doctor in here,"
he says.

"We will," responds Jimmy,
his surface appearance of someone
who has his shit together,
undisturbed even now, in the midst of this.

He's realising again
how it's not an act at all.
This is him.

VALKYRIE LOUGHCREWE

In action.
Living.
Not like the quiet moments,
when the doubts come creeping in,
the questions.

Cora steps away,
unnoticed.
Forgotten.
As Aaron starts to disinfect the wound,
and Saoirse starts to howl.

"What are they doing to her? Sonia . . . SONIA!!!"

Saoire's words resound in Cora's mind
that one phrase looping
on repeat
"we had to pull that THING into the world"
That THING
That THING
That THING

I don't know this woman
I don't know these people . . .

"They're putting her to rest, love,"
Cora hears Jimmy say.
She steps out of the door
and hears a chainsaw starting up,
somewhere down the farm.

And it all just reeks of cow shite,
as it so bloody often does.
She looks down the gravel path,
considering her options.

Flee, steal one of the cars.
Hitchhike? No, too dangerous, too frightening.

CROM CRUACH

Saoirse's calling out her name.
Her chest tightens, panic taking hold.

I don't wanna go back in there

"She needs you."
Goran's voice.
He's coming back toward the house.
Pale and sweating, shaken, shaking.
Staring at her, past her.

"Well I need to be outside right now."

Goran shakes his head, trying to ground
into the moment.

"Me too."

He tries to lean against the house,
but the pebbledash is too uncomfortable.
So he just stands there, crawling in his skin,
marinating in his life choices,
and the scope of their consequences.

"I don't trust her any more." Cora says.
"Any of you. I—"

Terry interrupts her, bursting out the front door.

"I'm going to get a doctor.
Jimmy's planning on swinging down
to Saoirse's dad's house."

"I'm going with him," Cora says,
taking herself by surprise.

"Cool, don't care," from Terry,
climbing into her car.

VALKYRIE LOUGHCREWE

"You were saying?" Goran says
the look in his eyes indicating,
that he's not really very interested,
in Cora's opinions at this time.
She feels heat rushing to her face,
and intense anger building.
She should leave,
but, she walks back into the house,
without another word.

She needs to know.

CHAPTER 15

A thin veneer of fog
shrouds Saint Patrick's Cathedral,
making Oisin acutely aware,
of just how unnatural the alien beauty
of its architecture is,
just jutting there between the hills.

A gravel road slices upward through
the boggy ground toward it.
Always just a month or two,
of lapsed maintenance away,
from sinking back into the soil.

There always has been something off about this place
as much as Oisin loves cathedrals, appreciates them,
this one has never really felt alive, or connected to the broader
spiritual community of the area.

Despite the occasional wedding, baptism or church choir concert,
people generally have always preferred
to worship at their local chapels.

Even those who live near this place,
frequent two churches in the nearest town,
Protestant and Catholic alike,
leaving this extravagant anomaly,
to sit largely in silence.

Who even maintains it these days?

VALKYRIE LOUGHCREWE

Before the war it was some dodgy corporate/government group,
and then it fell into the hands of Peadar Foley,
a weird young lad from up the town,
and a small army of old ladies.

But Peadar Foley's long past gone off to Portugal,
and Oisin never really knew any of the aul ones.
He regrets not stopping for conversation
on his previous visits to Saint Patrick's,
to marvel at the architecture,
to pray and meditate,
never quite feeling that connection
he would get in other,
similar spaces.

He never had any clue
that this spot had been so crucial,
in the foundation of Ireland's socio political trajectory.
He always thought it was just some weird,
forgotten extravagance, in the arse end of nowhere.

Maybe it's not the place that feels off,
he thinks, as he walks up the gravel driveway.

It's probably just me, out of place.
Out of touch with the community.
Never fully accepted by the pagans, being a christian and all,
Never fully accepted by the church folks, being black and dating
    a witch.
Not that I want to be accepted by racists and bigots,
but it'd be nice to belong somewhere
that isn't a monastery.

Stepping up to the entrance,
Oisin dips his fingers in the font.
He blesses himself, stepping inside.
The nave is quiet, and still,
the pews shining, polished,
but something is amiss.

CROM CRUACH

A smell, a hint of something,
like a pub, just after closing.
Sour, musty.

I wonder if I should have called someone.
Podge, Karl,
even Marco and Iarla,
in case this place
really does turn out to be harbouring
some kind of murderous cult.
But I don't wanna bother them,
waste their time,
following some esoteric hunch of mine.

At least I'm armed,
he thinks, noting the weight of the .45
in his coat as he walks on past the altar,
head on a swivel,
watching for movement.

He pushes through a door,
in the back, behind the altar
left unlocked.
Another smell hits him,
even harder than before.

Sweat, stale, like unwashed sheets,
like a living room on a hot summer's day,
where people have been hanging out,
doing nothing but watching TV,
and marinating in their sweat and farts.

The hallway looks normal.
Wooden floors, sparse walls,
undecorated other than the occasional
painting of Mary with the baby christ,
and a hanging crucifix.

I suppose they saved all of the opulence

VALKYRIE LOUGHCREWE

for the main hall,
Oisin thinks,
disappointed.

He'd expected artifacts and folk saints,
and depictions of Saint Patrick,
but the Irish country drabness
permeates above all.

The blandness-as-survival-mechanism,
of a chronically abused people,
extending even to the occupying religious order,
is a strange thing to behold.

Unsettled,
Oisin pushes through the doorway
where the musty smell
seems to be emanating from, and finds
a corner boarding room.

It's as spartan as the hall outside,
a single bed, a cupboard and a window.

And a grouping of sleeping bags
and backpacks on the floor.

Dim light falls upon the room,
a pale glow from behind thin green curtains,
The bed looks well used, the covers tousled.

A well worn copy of some old paperback
lies above the reeking sheets.

Oisin steps through the mess.
He notices
amongst the scattered clothes and bottles,
on the floor,
a combat knife,
brass knuckles too.

CROM CRUACH

His heart rate rising,
ears sharp, listening,
in case anyone's at home.

At the very least,
whoever these folks are,
they don't seem to reflect his own idea
of religious values.

The book upon the bed turns out,
to be something called
The Turner Diaries.
Well thumbed and yellowed pages.
Oisin's not sure what he's looking at,
He checks the back:

"The book which the FBI
and the controlled media have been
claiming hysterically is the 'blueprint'
for everything from the Oklahoma City bombing
to the takeover of the U.S. government by 'White extremists.'
It is the 'Bible' of the 'racist right'."

The blurb screams at him.
His blood runs cold.
It's nazis.
Of course it's fucking nazis.
When was it never nazis?

BUNF

A heavy impact from somewhere back in the building.
Like a door being swung,
a few rooms away.
In the nave maybe.
 Maybe the wind,
but Oisin's pulse is climbing
out of his throat,
and he isn't about to take a single bloody chance.

VALKYRIE LOUGHCREWE

It's a fair distance to the car,
and though he is armed,
a tiny handgun won't do much at a distance;

Fuck it.

Oisin climbs up onto the dirty bed,
brushes the curtain aside,
and tries the window.
Locked.
Oh shit.
Oh no.

He wonders about how wide he left
the door behind the altar open.
If someone could be creeping up on him,
without a sound,
so he turns back.

And for a long moment
he isn't quite sure what's happened.
His head swims.
He's facing where he thought the door was,
but it's the wood-paneled wall,
and the door is now off to his left.
But everything else, the placement of the bed, the window,
the sleeping bags,
are all the same.

Are they?
Did I mistake the layout of the room
on the way in?

A new smell pervades the muskiness.
A pleasant but heavy odour,
making Oisin's throat dry,
and his chest tight.
Frankincense
wafting through the misplaced wooden door.

CROM CRUACH

He wants to cough,
and someone coughs from inside,
hacking like a dying man.

This feeling comes upon him,
like a cooling, rushing water,
through his skull, soaking his brain.

A beckoning.

A feeling of being in the right place,
at the right time.
Something he felt once before,
during an ordeal the Franciscan brotherhood
put him through.

They deliberately infected him,
with pneumonia, and left him
in a stone chamber for a week
bereft of food and water.

It was the closest he'd ever been to the divine.

After days of pain and mania
That feeling came upon him,
and he could hear the water pouring,
from the distant gardens of heaven,
and he knew that this was right.
That everything was right.

And he remembers now,
that he's exactly where he needs to be,
and Dace, wherever she went,
She went in service of the highest good,
and love reigns true in the kingdom of heaven,
so he steps toward the misplaced door,
into the cloud of frankincense.

VALKYRIE LOUGHCREWE

A marble chamber.
Shining polished walls and ceiling.
At the farthest wall,
a statue of the archangel.

Oisin's heart sings at the sight
of the protector, the sword of
love and truth.
now here before him.
carved of deep obsidian,
with eyes of pearl and a shining
silver blade like nothing
Oisin's ever seen before.

Michael
plunging his glorious shining blade
into a writhing granite serpent
sculpted in eternal throes of pain.

There's a trail of fresh blood spattered
across the alabaster floor toward
Michael's feet.

A figure in black lies sprawling,
coughing, spluttering his last,
his head wrapped in purple velvet.

Oisin approaches, noticing
the discarded, night black, wide-brimmed hat
along the trail of blood.

He kneels, looking up to Michael.
Offers a prayer to the archangel,
as he undoes the velvet wrappings.

And looking down, he sees the pale, dying face
of Fintan Kavanagh
staring up at him.

CROM CRUACH

"They tortured me, Norrie," he wheezes.
"They tortured me.
Because I wouldn't . . . because I wasn't.
What year is this?"

"I'm not Norrie, Mr. Kavanagh," Oisin says softly.
"We need to get you to a doctor."

"Y-You were next." Fintan says,
his steel coloured eyes focusing,
recognising Oisin.

"Pardon?"

"You were supposed to be next . . .
But . . . she wouldn't act like he wanted her to . . .
Now it's all . . . out of order. "

Fintan laughs, coughing up bright red blood.
He looks up toward the statue.

"Out of order, you hear me, big man?"

Oisin starts to help Fintan up off the floor.

"Where are you injured?" he asks.
"Who did this to you?"

"Your girl came to see me,"
Fintan grunts
as Oisin heaves him to his feet.
The old man's words send a shock through Oisin's system.

"Dace? Dace came to . . . see you?"

Oisin doesn't notice Fintan,
taking a knife from his pocket,
but he feels it puncture him,
stabbing right into his stomach.

VALKYRIE LOUGHCREWE

It's a shock
but there's no pain,
just an acknowledgement.
That holy water pouring
all throughout his brain,
keeping him blissful,
if not utterly confused.

He watches, detached, as this old man,
suddenly full of strength and vigor,
tears into his abdomen
with leather, black-gloved hands.

Is this how I die?
Am I dreaming?
And Dace . . . Dace . . .
Where is she?
What happened to her?

He tries to speak,
but his mouth announces only gore.

"You've been good, brother Hall.
Yes. You've suffered for the lord.
And so I will award you a quick death."

"Dace . . . " Oisin manages to gurgle,
as the corners of his vision
begin to give away
to white hot, searing light.

The sun rising inside him.
Burning, cleaning,
annihilating self.

"You'll Meet Her In Heaven, My Son,"

CROM CRUACH

Michael says, through Fintan's mouth,
his voice a violent, disfiguring love,
as Fintan's hands pull Oisin's intestines out
in spools across the floor.

"Be Not Afraid."

INTERLUDE

CROM CRUACH

In a high, wild place of power, on a fog-strewn twilit hill,
a band of mortals stood amidst the brambles and the gorse,
and set out their rote petition for the valley dark beyond.

A chieftain, steely eyed and waning in the back half of his years,
gave the command to put the knife, then, to finest, fattest sow,
dig a cooking pit, call up a valley facing breeze,
to carry the intoxicating smell of cooking meat.

Steel Eyes,
his name and prior legacy lost to time,
only faint and disregarded visual impressions of his ghost,
remain alongside the bloody stain of his betrayal,
soaked into the waters of this island's stunted growth.

He beckoned the musicians to take up their tools and play,
their most accomplished masterworks,
keen and channelled compositions.
Sounds that seemed to wave upward and out from earth to sky,
compelling ease, humor, and blissful peace
to flower in the mind.

The fog parted like a corridor, all of a sudden to announce
the arrival of one whose steps echo beyond the mortal dance.
The place that seekers only glance,
where witches used to walk,
those ones who lived from flame to flame,
from torrid love to bloody war,
whose words and deeds alone could stir
the dreaming of the gods.

Dark hair wild and flowing, in it plants and fungi growing.
Clothing rough and formless shifting,
one metal limb-graft dully glinting.
Flesh shot through with bark and root,

VALKYRIE LOUGHCREWE

part earth, part human youth
parts woman, man, god, ghost and beast
equipped with bright sword, bow and shield.
Renowned for countless daring feats.

Face too beautiful to bear to see,
eyes innocent as a child,
yet full of danger, cruelty, and knowing,
the Hero from the wild.

Drawn there by the offerings,
that well tracked human gesture,
tasting again the damp, chill air of home.
Remembering humanity, its strife,
and how it feels to shape their lives,
and to be reshaped itself by consequence
in turn.

Steel Eyes' retinue prostrated,
preparing then the feast,
for of course the Hero,
keenly placed within the flow of time,
arrived just as the pig was thoroughly cooked
and thus ready to eat.

The supplicants cheered and gathered round
the ritual feast to dine,
bar Steel Eyes who stood back,
seemingly consumed in thought.

And those who dined upon the flesh were struck
by nerve-destroying spasms
first of limbs, then jaw, then heart and breath
poisoned, foaming, falling dead.

The Hero tried to stand, but even its legendary saol
could not stand against this draught.
Propping itself up upon the hilt of its bright and shining sword
it looked with desperate eyes and was met with only steel,

and a little golden symbol pressed against its dying cheek;
the Holy Roman Cross.

Steel Eyes spoke aloud
in a tongue foreign to the Hero,
but his meaning well implied:

For a new world to arrive,
the old one must first die.

Amen.

CROM CRUACH
PART THREE

CHAPTER 16

A blue Toyota Yaris sits parked
up along a bend in the road,
at a nettle-choked iron gate,
marking the border of a forest
at the edge of land maintained
by the group, known to some,
as the Morrighannain.

"What kind of evidence?" Iarla asks,
feigning interest.

His wife Yvonne's exasperated words
before he left with Marco—
taking her car, no less—
rattle through his mind.

"I dunno. Skulls?" Marco continues.
"Bits of clothes from the victims?
A voodoo altar
with their photographs on?
Anything that I can get to convi—
to prove their guilt."

Iarla is silent, too exhausted to respond.

"Or, what about the boy?
They might have the boy for their . . .
sodomy rituals
or whatever," Marco posits.

VALKYRIE LOUGHCREWE

"Jaysus," Iarla groans,
not needing that kind of imagery
in his head today.

"He won't help us where we're going,"
Marco intones gravely,
squinting out the window
like he thinks he's Dirty Harry.

"I guarantee you that."

A truck drives past them at speed.
Jimmy's pickup,
him and some pink haired queer
riding shotgun.

"Where are those faggots off to?"
Marco muses.

"Think they saw us?" Iarla asks,
feeling sweat prickle his brow.

"Didn't look like it," Marco responds,
not sounding very confident.

Iarla's phone buzzes.
Marco cringes as the lad fishes for it in his pocket,
instead of focusing on the task at hand.

"Jaysus," Iarla exclaims again.

Marco rolls his eyes,
temper rising.

"JohnEd found Gearoid."

"Alive?"

"He hanged himself in the woods, Marco."

CROM CRUACH

"Did he text you?"

"What?"

"JohnEd, did he text you about it?"

"Group chat."

"What group chat are you and JohnEd Smith in?"

"The fuckin' town alerts group chat. How are you not in it?"

"Don't get snarky with me."

"Stop acting like my dad, Marco, you're not my dad, and I'm not your fuckin' employee, alright? Those farmers don't have Gearoid. They're not satanists. There's no black magic. There's something else going on here and we have to work with them to figure out what's going on."

Marco huffs for a moment, eyes shut, chest clenched. Letting the rage pass over him before slapping the steering wheel.

"God damn it!" he cries, expelling his frustration. He starts the car and pulls onto the road.

"So what now?" Iarla asks.

"I'm going home, Iarla, how about you?"

Tentative relief begins to dawn

VALKYRIE LOUGHCREWE

as Iarla realises this could well be the end
of their little charade,
but is rudely interrupted,
by a frost-white SUV
careening around the corner
at far too high a speed.

No time to react, and even if there was,
that damn obnoxious vehicle,
is taking up the entire road.

The impact sends Marco,
never having been one for seatbelts,
slamming headfirst through the windshield,
one minute experiencing the pangs of self development,
the next a broken bloody doll,
of flesh and shattered bone.

***

"I'm sorry.
I'm sorry.
I'm so, so sorry"

Crawling from the wreckage,
blood streaking her blonde hair
Deirdre Ríordáin, fascist agitator,
clearly in a hurry to get as far from where she was,
as fast as bloody possible.

Gerry Rafferty's old white van
comes round the corner
to a stop behind Iarla's wife's car.
He leaps out and rushes to assist
the crawling, bleeding woman,
like a good old country boy.

"You shouldn't be moving hai, you're hurt," he says,
approaching Deirdre.

"I'll call for—"

CROM CRUACH

He's taken aback as she rears upward,
clawing at his clothes.
He sees her bruised eye sockets
and twisted broken nose.

"We need to go," she pleads, terrified.
"You need to get me out of here, NOW."

The door of Yvonne's blue Yaris opens.
Iarla, trying to struggle out,
dazed, trying to be proactive
but still buckled to his seat.

None of them notice the second white van
pulling up behind Deirdre's SUV,
mirroring Gerry's on the other side.
Or the man stepping out from the passenger side,
Balaclava clad, all in black,
Holding an assault rifle.

The kind of man who'd threaten a young woman
in front of a cathedral, and punch an older woman
in the face for talking back.

The man opens fire,
full auto swinging
from Deirdre
to Gerry
to Iarla,
and right across the car.

Relishing in the sound of breaking glass
and shredded metal.

He ducks back inside the van,
and vanishes as quickly as he came,
leaving nothing but slaughter and exhaust fumes
in his wake.

Howlings From New Babylon #35

Deirdre Riordain

HERE WE ARE NOW, YOU AND I, at the end of the slippery slope.

Fair Eire lies a-mouldering in her grave, and her once proud race are now a mongrel warlike kind.

Even I, a lifelong advocate of Freedom and National Purity, must admit that even the hated Royalists had a vision more noble than that of the wretched Marxist cabal that now enacts the Protocols of the Elders of Zion upon our Emerald Isle. I weep for their departure, as I weep for those of my Freedom Coalition which the "Republican Socialists" (I spit as I type those words) had shot and violated in dark alleys during the war which took our society from us.

Their final moments haunt me now. Shaking, frightened, praying "O Jesus O Mary save Ireland from the tyranny of the communist" as a pack of baying transracial gender abominations descended to make their final moments on God's Earth as close to hell as they could. I am hiding now on the fringes of the new anarchy, traversing the isles as best I can to evade the death squads, watching horror upon horror unfold before my eyes. As I watch the latest rape or torture from my latest fragile hiding place, words I never thought I would write keep rolling in my mind: I miss the Queen. I miss Britain.

By God, do I miss the church. The rosy smiles of the children on their way to prayer; the piety of the real traditional Irishman; the zeal of the priest as he endeavoured to guide his dwindling flock to salvation. When the children see them make speaking the name of God illegal in the coming years, they will know that they live in a fallen country, and that will make them fight. I know this. I pray to Jesus every night for the new generation to see through the lies of our own monstrous children and fight for tradition.

Dear reader, I implore you abjure the new slavemasters. They may be using friendly new names—Town Peace Coalition, Community Defence Associations, Rainbow Smile Foster Communities—but we all know who they really are: I.R.A terrorist lapdogs of the Merchant Cabal. To any Garda Síochana that may have survived the brutal purges, who may be reading this: hold strong. You are still the guardians of this nation, and the men of this country will overtake the pedophile socialist queers once more in due time, and return Ireland to God.

I must move on, my dear friends. There have been three child suicide bombings in one week of a quiet religious community I will not name, and I fear the firing squads are coming. You won't see anything about that in the Neo Soviet state media, but that's why you're a steadfast reader of this publication, isn't it? You seek the truth, and I, your humble scribe, shall continue to endeavour to provide it. So long as there is blood in my veins.

The white man marches on.

Tiochfaidh ar lá!

CHAPTER 17

"So. Are you gonna tell me or what?"
Cora manages to release the words
without a tremble,
a good start.

Jimmy sits in silence for a moment.
The radio plays some
mid '00s rap song,
as acres of young oak groves
pass them by.

"I'm tired of pretending I don't notice what's going on here.
And I need to know, cause frankly I've become scared of all of
      you.
Even Saoirse."

Jimmy remains silent,
a slight grimace on his face
the only indication that he hears her at all.

She thinks about all of the
true crime podcasts
she listened to in her youth,
and acknowledges the fact
that this could be the point of no return.

Still, she presses on,
realising how much this is still for Saoirse.

"And I wanna leave. But I need to know if I should or not."

VALKYRIE LOUGHCREWE

"Honestly," Jimmy says,
"You probably should.
I don't think this is going to end well for anybody.
The further away you are from this town
the safer you're gonna be."

"Jimmy," Cora says, her voice a stern monotone,
"What the fuck is going on?
What happened to Aaron's face?
Where the fuck did Dace go?"

A murmuration of crows appears over the horizon.
Jimmy takes a long, deep breath,
and decides, to hell with it.

"Do you know this county is the place where
Saint Patrick really broke the power of the
old indigenous magicians in the eyes of
the Irish Chieftains?"

"Yeah. Magh Slécht, Crom Cruach.
I have been living with you fuckers for a while."

"Right, so I suppose you know about that Cathedral as well."

"Saint Patrick's, that's where the Killycluggin Stone was broken.
Sacred spot, right? They built the cathedral there to . . . I dunno,
reclaim its power, right?"

"Aye, yeah. So, those church burnings, all over the country.
We figured because of them that things were changing,
and we live on a particularly important . . .
piece of that history.
So we decided to—"

"Burn down the cathedral? But it didn't work, did it—?"

"No."

CROM CRUACH

"—and, what, Crom, is—?"

"No.
No, listen to me. Believe it or not,
we didn't burn down that
wee chapel in Oldcastle."

"I don't."

"It's some other group.
Maybe the same ones who torched all those places in Leitrim.
We've been trying to get in touch with them,
figure out who they are,
but we can't.
Believe it or not, most people living here are more concerned
with how destroying local community focal points
will affect our relationship with said community,
then making big edgy statements."

"What are you saying? Could you get to the point?"

Jimmy sighs.
He's been dreading this.
They all have.
But it's clear that this can't stay buried.
Won't stay buried.

"We went to an area by the hill, by the cathedral, Killycluggin.
Middle of the night.
Lit a fire under some tree cover, dressed all in black.
Dace led the ritual to open the gates of Yesod,
and we all smoked DMT together.
We wanted to get in touch with that place,
the Chthonic,
Crom.
We wanted to get some kind of . . . confirmation . . .
that destroying the cathedral was the right thing to do.
Really change the minds of those on the fence. "

VALKYRIE LOUGHCREWE

Cora feels a helpless anger welling up inside.
She would never have let them do this.
If they had only bloody told her.
If only they had let her in.

"You idiots.
I knew this whole fucking secret magic club thing
was going to go bad.
What is it, a fae? A demon?"

"An angel," Jimmy says,
his voice quiet,
meek and frightened.
Like he's afraid of who might
be listening.

A cloud goes over the sun.
The temperature begins to plummet
as they take the turn onto the boggy road
toward Saoirse's father's house.

"Archangel Michael. He was waiting for us, he . . .
We knew as soon as we got there—to—
to heaven.
We opened the gate to heaven, Cora.
It was horrible.
It was like a graveyard.
It was like a weapons factory built
from bombed-out cities,
fueled by burning jungles.
And he . . . we saw him take over Dace, somehow.
She was the first to snap out of the trance . . .
She attacked Aaron,
pushed his face into the fire."

Cora sits in silence,
watching the top of Saoirse's father's
isolated house rise up over the hill.
Dark windows set in a deep blue facade.

CROM CRUACH

Her whole body buzzes.
She's unable to deny
what she can feel inside her gut
to be the hideous reality.

"In the struggle to get Dace off of Aaron,
Aidan . . .
Aidan went too far, and . . .
We killed her.
We killed Dace
and we buried her in the woods,
and we covered it up.
We promised never to speak of it again.
We promised we would go burn that cathedral down,
but we were scared.
I'm scared, to go back there.
And I've tried. I just . . .
I just can't do it."

Jimmy's truck sits there
in the middle of the crossroad.
he stops to check for traffic
before making the last turn
toward the house.

The first signs of groundwater
are leaking through the cracks
of the tarmac in the centre,
a job for the county council
lest the road be lost to nature.

The house on the hill sits obscured,
from this angle by tall ash trees,
hiding the garden and the house from prying eyes.

Fintan's always been a private man.

"I take it killing her didn't get rid of him." Cora says.

VALKYRIE LOUGHCREWE

"A few of us went out to check the gravesite last night.
It's empty."

Jimmy takes the turn toward the house.
They drive through the open gate, along the gravel path,
the house still hidden by the foliage.

"I don't . . . I can't believe this."

"After everything you've seen?
After the dead coming back to life? "

"I haven't seen anything like that.
I don't know what was wrong with Sonia, but—"

"She was dead.
It's not just us: *half the town* saw
Padraig and Lynda Boyle
moving around.
Lynda was missing her head, Cora,
and she was *singing*."

Jimmy stops the car,
words dead on his tongue.
The lower half of the house is burnt out,
One wall missing, windows shattered, door ajar,
A fire started and quickly extinguished.

Either that, he thinks,
but dares not vocalise,
*or a holy flame cut through the place,
The wrath of God upon them.*

CHAPTER 18

Aidan and Leanne run down a sloping field,
through overgrown grass left fallow for hay.
They're sore, exhausted,
and though the body they have just
dismembered was well past the point
of coagulation,
they still feel stained from head to toe
in Sonia's blood.

The sound of automatic gunfire
sent them running to investigate,
texting the others to stay inside,
that they've got this.

They find the cars, the bodies,
the blood and glass
on hot tarmac,
the van riddled with bullet holes.

"We're gonna be blamed for this!"
Leanne sobs.

"No, we're not."

"Aidan, Marco was accusing us of murder
and satanism in the pub last night.
that fucking woman—"

Leanne gestured at the blonde corpse on the road.

VALKYRIE LOUGHCREWE

"—is Deidre Ríordáin,
a famous bloody fascist sympathiser,
and they're dead right in front of our property
for some fucking reason?
We're fucked, man.
We need to hide these bodies, or—"

"No, no way.
I'm not doing this,
I'm done lying.
We call a meeting,
we lay out the truth."

"Are you crazy?" Leanne bellows.

"We leave out the shit about
the ritual and Dace and we just . . .
We tell 'em."

Leanne stares at him,
wide eyed,
like he's crazy,
as the sound
of a car engine
rumbles in the distance.

"Tell 'em what?"

He doesn't know
and the rumble's getting closer
pressure inside him at an apex,
it's time to make a choice.

"Fuck this," he exhales.
"I'm getting out of town. It's over."

Aidan turns
heads back toward the gate.

CROM CRUACH

"Aidan!" Leanne cries, dismayed.

"We've failed!" He bellows back,
leaving Leanne in the middle of the road,
surrounded by death.

CHAPTER 19

Jimmy steps across the threshold
into the darkened hall,
shotgun in his hand.
He winces at Sonia's blood
spattered across the wall,
and in dried, blackened streaks
upon the stairs.

Cora right behind him,
unarmed, looks up the staircase,
fearing the appearance of
some shadow or, worse still,
a blinding light.

"Fintan!" Jimmy calls out.
He barely stops himself
from calling out for Sonia too.

He sweeps into the living room
with its missing wall,
the ceiling there caved in.
Cora wonders if that's where Fintan kept his stash of booze,
if it exploded when exposed to fire.

"No bodies in here," Jimmy mutters.

"Would there even be?" Cora asks.
"Sonia walked away. Came after us."

CROM CRUACH

"Good point. We could have another one loose.
Or he could be alive."

He calls out again for Fintan, and is answered
by a sliding, muffled thumping sound,
coming from somewhere above their heads.

"That doesn't sound good."
Jimmy moves out into the hall
toward the stairs.

"Stay here," he says to Cora.

"No," she whispers back.

"Suit yourself."

Jimmy puts his weight
on the first step.
It creaks loudly
and he winces.

Cora looks back out the door
to make sure
nobody is approaching
from their flank.

All she sees is
a mundane gravel driveway
on an overcast country evening

It's dark up on the landing.
The curtains are drawn.
Nobody was around to greet the morning
when it came.

The attic hatch is open,
the ladder hanging half down.
Jimmy grimaces.

VALKYRIE LOUGHCREWE

Too much potential
for a sneak attack.

He exhales through his nose
and hands the shotgun to Cora.

"I'm going up. Cover me."

The weight of the weapon is heavy in her hands.
She's trained—a damn good shot too—
but she's never had to shoot anybody before.
Never even been in a fist fight,
but she's ready and half convinced,
anyway,
that whatever might lurch out of the darkness here
would not be human.

"Here," Cora says, reaching into her raincoat.
She hands over the switchblade
that Saoirse got her in Vietnam.
The pink one with the vampire ballerina motif.

He takes it,
unfolds the iridescent blade,
and pulls the ladder down,
ears sharp for any hints
of movement anywhere.

Heart pounding,
feeling the chill
from the uninsulated attic.
Jimmy takes hold of the first wooden rung,
and forces his body up toward
the dark hole in the ceiling.

The idea that he doesn't know
where the lightswitch is up there,
in the cold and dusty rafters,
does not help to ease the dread.

CROM CRUACH

He places the open switchblade
on the top rung of the ladder
and pulls his phone out from his pocket,
to activate the torch.
He hits the screen,
the light comes on.

Sitting there, illuminated,
splayed out, propped up, dessicated,

Dace
in torn, black,
mud caked robes,
a rusted broken sword
across her lap.

Eyeless sockets stare outward.,
Her once full, heart-shaped face,
now shriveled paper clinging to a lifeless skull.

Amidst the cardboard boxes,
cobwebbed antiques,
and other long forgotten things,
she's been waiting all this time.

Jimmy cries out,
shocked by the corpse
of his former high priestess,
and Cora,
despite her training,
despite her trigger discipline,
despite the fact that she's pretty sure
that she was *facing the bathroom door*,
fires the shotgun in shock
and hits Jimmy in the lower back.

The roar of the weapon deafens.
Ears ringing, overwhelming shriek.

VALKYRIE LOUGHCREWE

Cora sees Jimmy's body fall,
ragged wound in his back
where the shot tore cloth
and flesh
and bone.

She races to him, shakes him.
He's dead.
Her ears pulse with tinnitus,
her heart and head too full of
everything everything everything
that's happening,
and keeps happening.
Tears can't come.
Can't even feel.
Just staring at this dead man's face.

And she can't hear, but she knows that
something's crawling in that dark above,
toward her, nails scratching,
claws on wood and horrid laughter.

She turns,
looks up and points the gun
into that mouth of darkness.
The light goes out,
the darkness spilling
out from the attic.

The blackness overwhelming,
heavy, and she can feel it there
just out of sight
about to show itself.

As her eyes adjust
she thinks she sees a shape
up in the hatch.
Gun trembling,
she grits her teeth

CROM CRUACH

—and loses nerve.

She turns back to the stairs to flee,
and there's a man blocking her way.

Visceral shock floods through her system,
but she doesn't pull the trigger
'Cause she's trained, and
not a fucking idiot.

(Though Jimmy's corpse might disagree,
and hadn't she been facing a completely
different direction when she pulled that trigger?)

Three people are in front of her.
Behind the man, there stand two others.
JohnEd Smith, the butcher,
Sally Lynch, the teacher,
and Niall Tierny,
a young lad
from the CDA.

She sets the gun down:
"I-it was an accident."

JohnEd pushes her aside and rushes over
to check Jimmy.

"He's dead, oh Jesus christ you've killed him."

"You're not getting past us,"
Sally says,
misinterpreting
Cora's thousand mile stare
past her direction.

Cora sinks down to sit
on the top step,
catatonic.

VALKYRIE LOUGHCREWE

"There's something in the attic," she says.
"It made him scream and i-it startled me."

"You stupid fucking faggot!"
Niall exclaims
and lashes out
a kick right to her face.

"Hey!" JohnEd calls back to him.
Niall steps back onto the stairs.
He and Sally staring
hate-filled
straight at Cora.

Cora lies back, checking her teeth.
They're not broken, but
her jaw and neck ache.
She's too numb to feel afraid.
There's too much,
too much happening.

"Fucking JAYSUS!!" JohnEd calls out,
from the top of the attic ladder.

"It's that Polish girl, she's long dead—rotten!"

Cora feels a hand on her shirt.
The grip tightens, pinching her skin.
She's pulled up to her feet,
right up to a sneering face,
breath stinking like a compost heap.

"Why is there a missing woman's body in Fintan's attic?"
Sally hisses.

"Where the fuck is Sonia?" Niall chimes in.

Something stirs in Cora's heart.

CROM CRUACH

Her brain is grinding too much.
Horror too much.
Trauma cannot.
Think.
Just grey.
Static.

Let me speak

"Th—"

Yes That's It Let It Up
Let It Up
Open The Throat
Speak The Words

"They're a cult," she says.
"I've—they've been keeping me prisoner."

"I knew it." Niall spits.

Sally's grip upon her loosens.
Cora takes a step back.
JohnEd puts a hand upon her shoulder.

"Go on," he says, encouragingly.

"Dace . . . the—she led this ritual—
they . . . they
sacrificed her and
made Jimmy their—"

No i can't lie i can't do this no

"Their executioner . . .
h-he killed them . . . the Boyles . . . he was . . .
Fintan, Sonia, Saoirse,
he was t-tormenting them—
us . . . they all were."

VALKYRIE LOUGHCREWE

"That traveller bastard, I knew it," Sally mutters.

"Pagan and travellers. Scum." JohnEd spits.
"Did they burn down that church in Breifne, did they?"

Cora opens her mouth, her throat,
waits for the word to come.
They don't
so she forces them out.

"Yes."

CHAPTER 20

It hadn't taken long,
for Community Defence members
to arrive on the scene of the massacre.

Leanne called them as soon as Aidan departed.
If she didn't, somebody else would have,
and the Morrighannain would be left in a very
very
bad position.
She let them know where Jimmy and Cora were,
then they took Saoirse off to the hospital.

And then it was just herself, Terry and Goran,
standing in the wreckage.
Trying to theorise with the lads with guns,
as the clouds rolled in,
and the rain came down,
what might have happened?
Who might have done it?
What has befallen this town?

That woman clearly crashed into Iarla and Marco's car.
Maybe someone had been chasing her,
and then stopped to gun them down?

Had anybody seen any suspicious vehicles
that day?

VALKYRIE LOUGHCREWE

Group texts were sent out,
the town buzzing with suggestions,
though a lot of them, went more or less the same:
Those satanists on the farm in Breifne.
those church burners in our midst,
those who we see in strange places at night,
must have been the cause of this.

The group felt so small then,
without Dace, without Aidan,
Jimmy absent, she didn't realise
how few of them there really were,
when it came down to it.

How alien they were,
to the broader community,
outside of what they could grow,
and what they could trade.

"Look," Goran said to the CDA boys.
"You can pin it on us, but if you
take us out and it keeps happening,
what then?"

"It's not gonna come to that."
Eddie McMahon,
a young lad of barely twenty said,
though the rifle he was clutching
sent another vibe entirely.

"We'll catch them, don't worry,"
red haired Ciara Rahill said,
smiling directly at Leanne.
A long time customer,
of her homemade soaps and bath bombs.

But there was grumbling from the older lads,
who'd not known them all that well.

CROM CRUACH

"Take them in and question them.
We can't have them running free."

"It's obvious what's going on here.
Stop beating around the bush!"

And so it went until the news came in.
What they found in Saoirse's father's house.
What they found up at Saint Patrick's.
Oisin Hall, dead, eviscerated.
Gore strewn altar, desecrated.
The words
CROM CRUACH
writ large on the stained glass window in his blood.

Down the wire,
in black and white text,
came Cora's telling of events:

They are a cult

Plain to see for everyone in town.
Guns were drawn.

"Get on the ground!"

"The game's up, lads."

"I'm sorry," Sarah whispered
as she zip-tied Leanne's hands
behind her back.

MICROALGAL-BACTERIAL FORMATIONS AND THE STANDING STONES OF IRELAND

network insists that the oldest rock in the formations are fossilized human remains, this is being considered junk data, forming the centrepiece detractor's arguments against the belief

controversies around the findings as the radiological techniques, assisted with the use of the open source neural network known as

CARROWMORE

KILLYCLUGGAN

comprised of fossilized flora to a molecular degree not present in other forms of local

researchers believe this is what has given rise to "Spiral Clusters" in the atomic-to-subatomic structures, not at all dissimilar to the arranged structures of the stones on site, at least as far as the depart-

...deavours to dissociate the Druids from ...ractices, of which he says strangely there is "no ...." in Ireland, although there, as elsewhere in ...ca, Druidism was all-powerful. There is little ... however, that in Ireland also human sacrifices ... time prevailed. In a very ancient tract, the ...nchus," preserved in the "Book of Leinster," it ... that on Moyslaught, "the Plain of Adoration," ... a great gold idol, Crom Cruach (the Bloody ... To it the Gaels used to sacrifice children ... ng for fair weather and fertility—"it was ... n they asked from it in exchange for their ... great was their horror and their

a sampling of the so-called "Spiral Cluster found at

CHAPTER 21

Saoirse is alone,
staring up at the beige hospital ceiling.
Trying not to move too much,
to not jostle the IV drip in her arm.

Her head is sore.
Mouth is dry.
Slowly regaining her breath,
after crying herself out.
She's settling into an uneasy stillness,
accepting that the future that she built
together with her comrades
has been canceled.

She wonders about Ray.
If she should tell him about Dad
and Sonia.
It's been so long since they last spoke.
Over five years.

How would things have turned out?
If he hadn't left for Hong Kong.
With Da's bit on the side.
All those years ago.

If he had been around.
If he could have helped save Sonia . . .

She banishes the thought,

realising she's projecting blame
onto someone who isn't even in her life.

A knock at the door.
She lifts her head
and sees Cora standing there,
a sad, faint smile upon her face.

"Hey."

"Hey." Saoirse is surprised to feel
a genuine smile begin to grow.

With all that's going on,
with all that she has lost,
Cora's still here, right beside her.

Saoirse reaches out her arms,
unable to sit up.
Cora walks to the bed
and sits down delicately.

"I don't wanna—"

"Just avoid the IV and you'll be good."

She wraps her arms around Cora.
They hold each other,
Saoirse sighing as she lets her weight sink
into Cora's.
feeling her blood coursing,
the warmth of life still on her skin,
in the midst of all this death.

"I'm sorry," Cora says.

Saoirse's breath catches in her throat
She feels her face begin to buckle.
Feels tears about to fall.

CROM CRUACH

"Did you find my dad?" she asks.

"No.
Your house
was . . .
burned.
Like someone had burned out
the first floor and then, just,
put it out again, and . . . "

Cora stops herself,
changes tack.
If she spares some details,
maybe she can make this work.

"Th-they're holding . . . they've detained . . .
the remaining members of
the Morrighannain
in the old court house."

Saoirse freezes.

"Why?"

"Apparently there was a shooting,
outside the farm?
A lot of people died . . .
and . . .
everyone's convinced that you're—
we're—
the Morrighannain—
are satanists.
They're blaming everything on them."

"FUCK!" Saoirse screams,
pushing Cora away,
trying to sit up.
Feels her wound tearing open

and lies back with such force
that she slams her skull
against the bedframe.

"Of course, of course, yeah.
Okay, fuck it.
This is happening, this is . . .
This is what was always gonna happen.
This FUCKING WORLD IS YOURS OKAY!?
OKAY!?
YOU FUCKING OWN IT!!
YOU FUCKING OWN EVERYTHING DON'T YOU!!!"

She arches backward violently,
howling abjurations.

Cora grabs Saoirse by the shoulders
and hears people enter behind her.
CDA guards,
or doctors,
she can't tell.

She looks her lover in the face,
gets close, gives her a big smile.
Tears streaming down her face,
as Saoirse's eyes dart around,
her face a primal mask of rage.

"Listen to me," Cora says,
"they're giving us a choice.
Just you and me:
Leave
or face the trial,
face execution.
With the rest of them."

Their eyes lock.
Now's the moment of truth.
If the guards tear them apart,

CROM CRUACH

Cora wants them to hear Saoirse
acknowledge *her* version of events.

"I told them what happened, Saoirse.
How you weren't involved—*nor was I*—
How Dace and Jimmy manipulated us,
kept us silent and afraid."

Saoirse's expression shifts from
rage to abject horror,
realising what Cora is telling her.

What this means she has done.

"Come with me."
Cora smiles, so sadly,
tears dropping down
onto Saoirse's lips.

"Let's get out of here.
Let's start again,
somewhere else."

Time slows to a crawl for Cora,
Watching, hoping, screaming inside
for Saoirse's face of open mouthed terror,
to soften into a sad smile of acceptance.

A kiss, or just a nod.

Anything.

Saoirse's face contorts in rage.
She struggles to form the words.
They come out in a rasp.

"I'm staying."

Cora feels the sorrow rising

fast up to her face, and so she
gets herself up off the bed,
and looks back to the
door.

Whoever was there now is gone.

"I didn't fight for this world to have it
taken away from me by a lie,"
Saoirse spits.
"And whoever is behind it all
is still out there!"

"Saoirse—"

"I'm not leaving."
Saoirse growls,
"I *am* this place.
I *am* Cavan.
I'm staying
and I'm telling the truth."

"They'll kill you."

Saoirse looks Cora dead in the eye,
her face grim, set, eyes burning.
Face like a wrathful deity.
Face like a fallen angel.

"Do you think that will fucking stop me?"

A chill breeze comes through the window.
Cora looks away, down at the linoleum floor.

"We found Dace."

"Did you destroy her?"

"They're gonna bury her."

CROM CRUACH

Saoirse closes her eyes and lies back in her bed.

"Go. Leave town.
Go live your life."

"Saoirse, I love you."

Saoirse sighs bitterly.
She wants to hurt Cora,
wants to send her away
with a splinter in her soul
that will hurt her for the rest of her days.

But what the fuck's the point in that?
"Yeah. I love you too," she says.

"Now just . . .
 fuck off, okay?"

CHAPTER 22

The sun comes down over the farm.
Cora rumbles up the driveway,
in the rusted old banger
that the CDA provided her
to get out of town.

Unsure where to go,
maybe straight toward the sea.
Get a boat to somewhere else,
Spain maybe?
Maybe Finland.
Somewhere new.

Fortune meets her at the door,
meowing angrily; it's feeding time.
She sighs and steps into the house.

Dusky golden light
is shining through the door.
It highlights Saoirse's blood,
dried and darkened on the floor.

She moves on through the living room,
along and past the trail of blood.
Through to the kitchen, noticing,
all of the instruments, the records,
artworks, clothing,
owned by so many different people
who once lived here, on and off.

CROM CRUACH

United by a common goal,
a need to build a world,
more altruistic than the one
they fought and killed for.

The cat mews inquisitively,
sensing something different.
Cora reckons she will take her.

She finds the kibble in the cupboard,
and fills a bowl at the back door.

Wondering now what's going to happen
to the cows, the goats, the chickens.
Others probably will move in and take over,
unless they leave the place to rot
in superstitious fear.

She wonders if the trial is happening now.
If Saoirse's standing there before the town,
telling them what happened,
about the angel,
about the ritual,
about Aidan.

She wonders if they'll believe her.

And if they do, what happens to me then?
Is it worth sticking around for,
to be the traitor who would have
gotten everybody killed for her own safety?

She sends herself up the staircase,
toward the room she had shared
with the woman she has
put to death.

VALKYRIE LOUGHCREWE

Still a mess.
But aired out somewhat
from the window left ajar.

She sits down on the bed,
her mind empty of what it is
she needs to take with her
on her journey.

Phone, computer, enough clothes to last a wee
What's that?   *eist*
Strange   *maithiúnas*
    a
Some kind of buzzing   *habhairt duit*
In her head like someone's
operating machinery outside.

She tries to shake it off,
waits for it to fade, but it only   *caithfidh tú*
increases in intensity.
It's loud now.   *a bheith toilteanach*
Deafening.
Like it's coming from inside her head.
There's a rush of force from right in front of her,
like hands pushing her down.
It sends her slamming back   *a mharú*
onto the bed.

Standing,
looming over her,
a pale and rotting hag.

Eyes ice blue and burning,
like candles in a jack o' lantern.
Horror grips her, she's paralysed
as the thing begins to whisper
not in words,
but images.

CROM CRUACH

A woman, underground.
A giant, sleeping, her face a grimace.
Her hair, water running upward
through the rocks,
crystalline spring,

A blockage, near the surface.
The foundations of a church.

The water turning to sludge
and flowing back down, causing distress
to the placid deity
beneath the earth.

And in the church, a mound of bodies,
butchered,
an endless charnel pit.
The freshest corpses at the top:
the Boyles, Sonia, Fintan, Oisin.

From the rafters,
choking on nooses made of their own intestines
are the Morrighannain
as holy light shines downward
through the permeable ceiling.

Between the shining roof above,
and the death choked earth below,
a group of men with the heads of wolves
revel in the carnage.

Dancing, chanting, raising chalices of blood.
Toasting to the destruction of their victims.
Howling zealously, as the white light from above
sears their flesh, bubbles and blisters . . .

***

VALKYRIE LOUGHCREWE

Cora
lying in the bed
drenched from head to toe in sweat
alone once again in the room.

Feels a rage burn in her chest
and she thinks she understands
for the first time in her life
there is an act that she can do
to make a difference in this world.

She sits bolt upright
and looks toward the wall
at Saoirse's rifle.
She smiles a wicked smile
as tears cascade from bloodshot eyes.

CHAPTER 23

The neophyte has been blooded.

His blade had been the first,
to penetrate the flesh
of the young girl in the house.

The house his own hand burned.

The mission is complete.
The heathens caught like rabbits
in a trap, awaiting final judgement,
and their doom.

The cathedral has been cleaned,
as was their duty as its keepers.
The signage and the caution tape
keeps others out.

They gather round, the six of them,
by candlelight, victorious,
resplendent in their wolf-skins,
strong and proud.

Apart from The Boy,
soon to become a man,
standing naked in the centre
before his last final initiation.

VALKYRIE LOUGHCREWE

Brother Engvir
(also known as Darragh, to his mammy)
hands the boy
the skinning knife and motions him
toward the cage
in which the she-wolf lies sedated,
imported from a farm

(though they told the boy they caught
her while out hunting in the woods)

Brother Prestrvald,
up at the altar,
speaks his sermon
as the boy approaches, opens the cage,
and drags the panting animal out
onto the marble floor.

"This is a shining moment,
in the history of our order,
another parish returned to
the love and fear of God,
another Ulfhednar to join
our merry ranks.
The prey is ours!
The hunt is a success!"

The she-wolf shudders,
too tranquilized to shriek
as the boy begins to peel
her fur and skin away.

"Strip the bitch's flesh, my boy.
Show God your mastery.
Over the beasts.
Over the cunts of this world.
Overpredator, you are.
More than wolf.
More than man."

CROM CRUACH

He pulls the dripping
pelt back, trying his hardest
not to gag.

I'm tough, he tells himself.
I love this shit.

He forces himself to laugh
as he feels the creature's muscles
strain to keep the skin attached.

The men around begin to chant,
opening their throats and
howling out the ancient words
of their sacred tribe

(Words that definitely weren't cooked up
by a t-shirt company in the mid-nineties
to peddle Valknut merch)

He skins the pelt up to the head,
and begins the final stage,
to saw away the creature's lower jaw
and place her head atop of his.

To stand there in the running blood,
and scream his first cries,
reborn as *Ulfhednar.*

The chanting reaches apex volume.
Bestial roars, now barely words.
Awaiting the climax where they will
all howl together as a pack.

They do not hear the doors creak open,
or the step of combat boots
across the marble of the nave,
as a young transgender woman

VALKYRIE LOUGHCREWE

marches up along the pews,
an AK-47 in her hands
and a grimace on her face.

Darragh sees her first
and calls out, but his scream
is lost in the furore.
He's the first one that she shoots.

She feels the gun jump in her hands,
thinking how close this makes her
and Saoirse now,
both having cut down fash with the same gun.

She doesn't break stride.

She pitches the muzzle of the weapon down
across the wide eyed men
dressed in their viking LARPer gear
and opens fire, grinning.

Fully automatic,
screaming, cackling rage
of something from below the earth
flooding outward from her throat,
and from the barrel of her gun.

She arcs the bucking weapon,
making every bullet count,
ripping through the flesh and bone
of the men who took her life away.

***

Further up the road,
as far away as town,
a firing squad of reluctant people
let rattle out a volley.

CROM CRUACH

The gunfire cuts down a number
of their long-known friends and neighbours
for reasons rapidly becoming
less and less coherent.

"It had to be done" they will say
for years and years to come
blaming what comes next on Aidan,
the one that got away.

***

From her car, Cora carries out
a canister from the barn.
Splashes fuel over the pews
and the bodies and the altar
and the curtains
and the crucifix
until the can runs dry.

She goes back out,
grabs herself another fucking can,
and does the very same again.

The cathedral reeks of gasoline.
Cora can barely breathe.
She retreats outside the doors and
takes in a breath of cool night air.

The lights of the town beyond,
The houses on the hills
twist her stomach,
fill her with hate,

These people who would have sleepwalked
humanity into extinction,
who needed to be dragged
kicking and screaming into
a new type of reality.

VALKYRIE LOUGHCREWE

And those others
who she thought were different,
playing around like children
with forces far beyond
their control or comprehension.

For the sake of such a petty gesture
as the incineration of a pointy fucking house upon a hill.

She breathes in another gulp
of kerosene-corrupted air,
and wishes she could see something.
Anything that would confirm,
that what she's doing is correct.

The hag again, some eldritch omen,
some concrete sign to show that the spirits of this place
are free at last.

But nothing shows its face.
Nothing whispers on the wind.
So she turns back to face the church,
and lights the match.

She thinks there to herself,
just before she hurls the flame:
*Even if this whole experience
has been of no true greater worth*

*At the very least this night,
by the actions i have taken
There are six less fucking nazis
on this motherfucking earth.*

ABOUT THE AUTHOR

Valkyrie Loughcrewe lives in a bog, and is currently at this moment working on something gory and crawling with nightmare creatures. Whatever you do, don't look them up on twitter—in fact, don't look anyone up on twitter. Start raising homing pigeons!

Val also makes diabolical industrial electro music under the name Surgeryhead and gnarly death thrash metal as Argento!

CONTENT WARNINGS

ABOUT TENEBROUS PRESS

Tenebrous Press was conceived in the Plague Year 2020 and unleashed, howling and feral, in spring 2021 to deliver the finest in transgressive, progressive Horror from diverse and unsung voices around the world.

We welcome the esoteric; the unorthodox; the finest in New Weird Horror.

FIND OUT MORE:
www.tenebrouspress.com
Twitter: @TenebrousPress

NEW WEIRD HORROR

www.ingramcontent.com/pod-product-compliance
Lightning Source LLC
Chambersburg PA
CBHW030956210726
48290CB00007B/2343